Maid of Dishonor

Maid of Dishonor

A Wedding Bell Mysteries Novel

Nancy Robards Thompson

Maid of Dishonor
Copyright© 2024 Nancy Robards Thompson
Tule Publishing First Printing, July 2024

The Tule Publishing, Inc.

ALL RIGHTS RESERVED

First Publication by Tule Publishing 2024

Cover illustrated by Cortney Langevin Spillane

No part of this book may be used or reproduced in any manner whatsoever without written permission except in the case of brief quotations embodied in critical articles and reviews.

This is a work of fiction. Names, characters, places, and incidents are products of the author's imagination or are used fictitiously. Any resemblance to actual events, locales, organizations, or persons, living or dead, is entirely coincidental.

AI was not used to create any part of this book and no part of this book may be used for generative training.

ISBN: 978-1-964703-12-1

Dedication

This book is dedicated to my daughter, Jennifer.
You are amazing and so very loved.

Praise for Nancy Robards Thompson

"Robards Thompson's sense of emotion is keen."
—Publishers Weekly

"Details are brilliant. Readers can look forward to seeing how Robards Thompson's talent develops."
—Library Journal

"Funny, smart and observant, Thompson writes with charm and flair."
—Romantic Times BOOKreviews

"Ms. Thompson's novels are a sure winner in the eyes of this reviewer."
—Love Romance

"Ms. Thompson has found a way to speak to the heart."
—Romance Reviews Today

If you are looking for a fun, enjoyable read filled with fabulous characters-pick up Slay Bells Ring!
—Sue ~ Amazon

A page turner that keeps you guessing.
—Nana ~ Amazon

Fun cozy mystery read which pulled me in from the beginning.
—Denise ~ Amazon.

Chapter One

~ *Maddie* ~

THE SHRIEK REVERBERATES through the corridors of Gracewood Hall like a banshee portending death. I drop the ringbearer's pillow, which I'm sewing, and sprint toward the caterwauling.

"Why are you not wearing the nail polish I asked you to get, Betsy?" Bride-to-be and social media influencer London Brinks screams at her maid of honor.

Betsy stares at her glossy, deep green nails for a moment before she opens her mouth to answer, but London steamrolls over her.

"Did I or did I not explicitly tell you to buy Les Mains Hermes nail enamel in *Vert Egyptien*?"

London's Southern accent murders the French words and Betsy smirks at her defiantly.

My daughter Jenna stands between them, arms bent at the elbows, palms out, like a boxing referee keeping the fighters apart. She glances at me as I skid to a stop in the doorway.

"London," Jenna says. "Even if it's not Hermes, the nail polish Betsy is wearing will look lovely with her dress."

That is if one likes the color green.

London's face turns a cartoonish shade of deep red. I'm starting to worry that her head might explode when my mother, Gloria Phillips—everyone calls her Gigi—appears on the threshold next to me.

"What's all the ruckus about?" she asks.

I put a finger to my lips and nod toward the action, determined to let my daughter take care of her clients.

Gigi owns Gracewood Hall, the venue. I own Blissful Beginnings Bridal Boutique. Jenna owns Champagne Wedding and Event Designs. Despite my mothering instincts to step in and make everything right, I know I must stay in my lane. Jenna is more than capable of handling the situation.

"I said Hermes because I want Hermes." London's voice is guttural and low, shaking like a volcano ready to erupt. "What is so difficult to understand about that?"

Gigi, who could be Betty White's younger sister, returned to Hemlock, North Carolina, last year after her fourth husband passed away. It's good to have her home. I'm glad she turned to us in her grief.

She's outlived all of her husbands and admits she's starting to feel like a black widow—even though they all died of natural causes, and she had nothing to do with their deaths. She doesn't want to get married again, but she still believes in love. So, she purchased Gracewood Hall, the storied mansion on a sprawling property on the outskirts of Hemlock, North Carolina, and turned it into a romantic wedding venue.

Hosting London Brinks's wedding as Gracewood Hall's inaugural event was Gigi's idea.

I would outfit the bride and groom.

Jenna would plan the wedding and reception.

Gigi would host the wedding—the first event at the newly renovated and reopened Gracewood Hall.

London Brinks would post about the event on her social media accounts, and her three million followers would clamor to book their weddings and events here, too.

Little did we know.

"I don't know what kind of skank-show weddings you coordinate, Jenna; my followers expect better than a low-rent imitation of my brand."

Despite my resolve, I start to step forward, but Gigi puts a hand on my arm, holding me back.

"We agreed my wedding would be classy, which means first-rate everything, right down to the Hermes nail polish. What is that tackiness on your fingers, Betsy? Don't tell me it's OPI."

"As a matter of fact, London, it is OPI." Betsy rolls her eyes. "It's called *Stay off the Lawn!!* And that's with two exclamation points. You are a piece of work."

"No, Betsy, you are," London yells. "You agreed to my

standards when I let you be in the wedding. It was all good when you thought you'd get exposure at my expense—"

"How is anything at your expense?" Betsy yells back. "You get everything free. You get to wear the twenty-thousand-dollar bridal gown at no cost. You get the sixty-dollar Hermes nail polish free, but you expect me to go out and drop a fortune on a dress in a hideous shade of chartreuse that I will never in my life wear again. And then when I try to save a few bucks on nail polish, you treat me like a criminal."

She's right—the dress is chartreuse. While it's a fun, trendy color, it doesn't flatter many people—certainly not Betsy, with her brassy blonde hair and pale skin. The color makes her look like she's nauseated.

"By the way," Betsy adds. "The Hermes nail polish doesn't even match the chartreuse dress."

"Get a manicurist in here right now," London barks at Jenna. "Have her redo Betsy's nails. I suppose she will have to use my bottle of Hermes since Betsy was too cheap to spring for a bottle of her own. If the manicurist charges, send the bill to her."

"Jenna, don't bother," Betsy says. "I quit. I've put up with her verbal abuse for months, and I'm done. I don't care if she is marrying my brother. I should've dropped out when the rest of the bridesmaids walked out on her, but I figured since I was the last woman standing, she'd get a clue and rein it in. No more. I've had enough."

"Oh, no," Jenna says. "Betsy, the wedding is in two days. Please don't go. London has pre-wedding jitters. She needs you more than ever right now." Jenna casts a pleading glance at the bride. "Right, London?"

"I don't need you, Betsy." London crosses her arms and turns her back on them. "Go on. Get out of here. Just *get*."

As London shoos her away with a swatting flick of her hand. Betsy picks up the garment bag that holds the bridesmaid dress. She shakes her head and mutters, "I am so out of here. I'm so over this."

While Jenna deals with London, I go after Betsy, hoping to convince her to change her mind and stick it out.

"Betsy, please don't go. It's your brother's wedding. Hang in there for two more days."

With one hand on the iron rail, Betsy stops at the top of the marble staircase leading down to the grand foyer and heaves a weary sigh. She looks exhausted, and I can feel the frustration emanating from her in waves.

We can hear London shrieking out here.

"Now, what am I supposed to do?" London wails. "Everyone is against me. Every single person who agreed to be in this wedding was doing it for the exposure they'd get on my social channels. They're all a bunch of users. I hate them. I hate them all."

"See what I mean?" Betsy says. "Would you want to stick around for two more days of that abuse? Oh, I'm sorry. I forgot you have no choice."

I weigh my words because I am firmly on Betsy's side. She's right. Jenna, Gigi, and I don't have a choice.

It's good that my daughter is handling London because I want to tell the spoiled brat to take a long look in the mirror. If she thinks the whole world is against her, the entire world might not be the problem.

Jenna is handling her, saying something in a low, soothing tone that I can't discern.

"London Brinks might be Insta-famous, but she is a monster. I truly think she would kill her mother if it would get her ahead."

"Honey, don't say that," Gigi says. "She just wants her big day to be perfect. Or at least the version of perfect she sees in her mind's eye."

"Good luck with that. Now, she won't have any bridesmaids. That's because no one can stand her. Sure, she's a social media influencer, but if people knew the real her… You saw how she acts. She has no regard for anyone. Green isn't my color. But she chose the dress and expected me to drop a grand on it like it was pocket change. I will never wear that dress again, but she doesn't care. She thinks it looks rich and regal, but it's hideous. I can't do it anymore, Maddie. I'm out."

I feel bad because I sold her the dress, but I thought everyone was on the same page. London would borrow a dress, and the bridal party would pay for their own. But Betsy is right. Even after I gave her a substantial discount, the maid of honor dress that London picked out still cost more than $1,000.

"How about if I refund your money and let you borrow the dress for the day?" I ask.

London picks that moment to come charging out of the room. "Give back the bracelet, you nasty little thief."

Betsy shrinks away, but London grabs Betsy's arm and yanks the golden rope bangle off her thin wrist. The force of London's manhandling causes Betsy to teeter on the top step. I grab her arm to steady her. The last thing we need is someone to take a spill down the stairs.

"Be careful," I say. "If you two don't knock it off, someone will get hurt."

London ignores me and unleashes the enormity of her wrath on her sister-in-law-to-be.

"Don't you dare show up at any of the wedding festivities. If you do, security will throw you out. I don't care if Anson is your brother. Since you are abandoning me, you're not allowed to darken my big day with your ugly presence."

"Yeah, well, I can't believe my brother would marry someone like you. You're the ugly one. You'd probably sabotage your own wedding for the publicity."

London swats away Betsy's words, turns, and stomps back to the bride's room.

Betsy's brows raise, and she shakes her head. "You heard her. If I show up, she will have security escort me out of my brother's wedding. I'd appreciate it if you would refund my money and let someone else beg, borrow, or steal the dress. I'm done."

She hands me the garment bag and walks down the stairs.

I turn and see Gigi standing there with her hands on her hips. She and I stare at each other.

"Well, seeing that neither of us is a size two, do you know where we can find a tiny stand-in who looks good in this strange shade of green?" Gigi asks.

I shrug, and we both head back to the bride's room, where Jenna talks to London in low, earnest tones. Miracle of miracles, bridezilla seems to be listening.

"Think about it, but don't take too long," Jenna says. "You're lucky she's free this weekend."

"What does she look like?" London asks petulantly.

Jenna holds up her phone and shows a picture of an attractive petite blonde.

London takes the phone and paces as she scrutinizes the image. "She's pretty and little. Maybe she's too pretty. My maid of honor can't be more attractive than I am. I might look like a moose standing next to her. You should know that, Jenna."

As Bridezilla scowls at the picture, I realize London isn't unattractive. She is big-boned and a little horsey-looking, which generally wouldn't even enter the equation because I don't judge women on their looks, but London is the one who brought up the potential replacement bridesmaid's looks.

Who is this person that Jenna's recommending? If London doesn't know what she looks like, Jenna must be suggesting someone to take Betsy's place as maid of honor.

Why should London be worried? She's one of the world's top social media influencers. She's not beautiful, but she makes the most of what she has. This, paired with her ease on camera, makes her relatable and approachable to her followers.

I wish I could pull her aside and tell her that while her online personality is friendly and helpful, her real-life disregard for others' feelings makes her unattractive.

"London, look," Jenna says in a steady, neutral voice. "Unless you know someone who can drop everything and come to Hemlock by tomorrow morning, you're out of options."

London bleats a *meh*, and with a flick of her wrist, she skims Jenna's phone back to her across the table. "I don't know."

My daughter barely catches it, saving the cell from sailing off the other end and smashing into the wall. I catch a barely perceptible flash of anger in my daughter's eyes.

Jenna takes a deep breath before saying, "Of course, you don't have to have attendants. You could walk down the aisle solo and say it's the new trend, but it might look a little unbalanced since Anson still has ten groomsmen."

"You haven't told him that he needs to get rid of at least

nine of them?" London bellows. "You were supposed to have already taken care of that. What in the world am I paying you for?"

"You're not paying me, London." Jenna's voice is devoid of emotion, and I know my daughter well enough to realize it's taking every ounce of strength she possesses to keep from throttling this woman. "We negotiated an in-kind trade. Promo for services."

"Go tell him that he has to let everyone go," London insists.

Jenna closes her eyes and rubs her temples.

"Oh, dear," Gigi whispers.

"Before I do that, we need to figure out what you're going to do," Jenna says. "Do you realize it'll raise some eyebrows if you don't have at least one bridesmaid?"

"But you said I didn't have to have a bridesmaid."

"I'm saying one attendant makes a statement, but flying solo at your first wedding suggests something is wrong, especially since you have five flower girls and two ringbearers.

"You can get away with not having an attendant if you elope or have a small gathering, but when you invite five hundred people to a wedding, it's bound to raise some questions if the bride has no bridesmaids. People talk, and by people, I mean the ladies you've kicked out of the wedding."

Yes, five hundred people are invited to the wedding. Gracewood Hall can handle it, but we will burst at the seams.

"Everyone in the bridal party signed nondisclosures," London says. "They can't talk, or I will sue them."

Jenna levels her with a look that says, *yeah, right*.

The real story is bound to get out. Even if London embraces the theory that there's no such thing as bad publicity, it won't be a good look. It could damage London's brand.

That must be what the woman thinks because I sense her bravado wavering.

London makes a clucking noise. "It seems so gauche to hire someone to pretend to be your friend."

I have to bite my tongue to avoid saying, "Well, honey, you've driven everyone else away. At this point, you're out of options."

But there is a note of vulnerability in her voice.

My diplomatic daughter says, "It's not gauche. It's a practical decision. You will be paying her to eliminate the drama. You want her to wear green Hermes nail polish? Consider it done. What do you say? Do you want to hire Kate for your big day?"

"What do you mean I'll be *paying* her?"

"Her services aren't free," Jenna says.

London makes a face that suggests this is the most ridiculous thing she's ever heard.

I'd heard about bridesmaids for hire, but I'd never known anyone who'd used the service. Jenna had resources and had already started looking into the possibility.

"You'll have to pay her because she doesn't do work in exchange for promo," Jenna explains. "She has to be discreet. Think about it. If you promote Kate's business, you'll tell your audience you hired your maid of honor."

London blinks. Reality seems to be dawning.

"I can vouch for Kate. I went to college with her. She's a professional. Whatever backstory you all come up with—whether she's your lifelong bestie or your sorority big sister, she will make everyone believe it's true. So, do you want to hire her to be your maid of honor?"

~ Jenna ~

LONDON RELENTED, AND I booked my friend Kate Asher as her stand-in maid of honor.

The next morning, I wait outside on the cobblestone driveway of Gracewood Hall for Kate to arrive.

I wince at the thought of throwing my friend to the queen of the bridezillas, but I remind myself that this isn't Kate's first rodeo. She will be well compensated for the trouble at $3,000 for the weekend, plus travel expenses and accommodations. While the job of bridesmaid for hire isn't for the faint of heart, one advantage that Kate has as a professional is there's no emotional baggage that potentially strains family relations or ruins lifelong friendships when a bride goes off the rails.

Still, London is a quirky little item who has proven she can test the outer limits of the strongest individual. This week, I watched her systematically decimate her bridal party.

Yesterday, I clarified to London that Kate was her last option. If she drives her away, she's on her own.

I draw in a breath of humid midmorning air.

Two more days.

Granted, two very long days, but if we can get through this wedding without the bride killing someone, I will have gained the skills that will enable me to handle anyone.

I will be invincible.

Heh.

If I say it enough, maybe I'll start to believe it.

A black sedan passes through Gracewood Hall's stately wrought iron gates. The Breedon Golden Amber gravel crunches under the car's tires.

When my grandmother, Gigi, bought the place last year and had it renovated, she insisted on only the best of everything. No shortcuts. No substitutions. If Breedon Golden Amber gravel was good enough for Buckingham Palace, it was exactly what she wanted for Gracewood Hall. I have to give her credit; it gives the place an understated regal air.

When the car stops in the circle part of the driveway, I walk around to the driver's side door to greet Kate.

"Look at you standing out here like you're part of the *Downton Abbey* cast," she says as she glances around in awe.

"Would that make me nobility or part of the waitstaff?"

We laugh and hug each other.

Kate is blonde, tan, and gorgeous. She's tiny but holds herself with an air of self-possession that makes her seem significant. It's a vibe that draws people to her while allowing her to keep them at arm's length.

I always likened Kate to an iceberg. She's ice-queen calm on the surface, but her natural strengths are hidden. I know this because while I considered her a friend, I never really knew her.

"It's been too long, Kate," I say. "I'm so glad you could come on such short notice."

"I'm happy to be here. I guess the wedding planning business is lucrative in these parts, huh? Clearly, I got into the wrong nuptial niche."

"Maybe not *this* lucrative." I gesture toward the house. "But I do okay. My grandmother bought this place last year when she moved back to Hemlock. Where's your luggage?"

"I checked into the hotel before coming here," Kate says.

Of course, she did. She's as efficient as I remember her.

She shades her eyes from the sun and gazes up at Gracewood Hall.

"So, how big is this place?" she asks.

"Big," I say. "I've never really counted the rooms beyond the ones used by the wedding party, the offices, and my suite."

Kate gives me a double take. "You live here?"

"I do. When Gigi bought the place, she decided it didn't

make sense to have a house this big and buy a smaller one to live in. She asked me to move in with her. When she renovated the place, she built separate apartments for us within Gracewood Hall."

I shrug and stop short of telling her that previously I'd been living in the downstairs apartment of my mother's house. When Mom got engaged to Hemlock's police chief, I needed to get my own place, so the move to Gracewood Hall made sense.

It wasn't as if I was twenty-seven and living in my mother's basement ... and so what if Kate took it that way? My mom is one of my best friends. I genuinely like being around her. That's why it's so nice working with her.

The business arrangement was a lot like our former living arrangement. We each have our own companies, but the businesses often intersect since she owns a bridal boutique and I own a wedding and events planning service.

It works.

I wouldn't feel compelled to explain myself if it were anyone other than Kate.

"I firmly believe Gigi saw how much fun we were having and bought Gracewood Hall so she could have a stake in it, too. Mom outfits the bridal parties. I plan the events. Now, Gigi provides the venue."

"Wow, you all are a triple threat." Kate trains her gaze on me and smiles. "I love strong women. You know this place has quite a history, don't you?"

I nod.

"I have to be honest with you," Kate says. "I was booked this weekend, but when you told me the location of the ceremony, I got a colleague to sub in at the other wedding for me. It's not every day you get full access to Gracewood Hall."

"I had no idea you were a Carter Stanton fan," I say. "Kate Asher, if I didn't know you better, I might think you were a romantic."

It's true. Gracewood Hall does have a romantic yet tragic history. Movie star Carter Stanton was making a film at the Biltmore estate when he met Linda Conti, a waitress at a diner in downtown Asheville. It was love at first sight. After a whirlwind romance, the two married in June of 1944.

People loved them together. Linda was the perfect *every woman*. If a man regarded as American royalty could fall in love with her, it could happen to every woman.

The couple spent their honeymoon at Gracewood Hall.

The legend goes that Linda fell in love with the place, and Carter bought it for her. They were going to live there and raise their family. Sadly, their fairy tale was short-lived. Soon after their honeymoon, Carter joined the war and died in the battle of Normandy later that year.

After his death, Linda moved out but couldn't bring herself to sell the place. So, it sat vacant until her death last year. Her estate wanted to sell it. Gigi knew someone who knew someone, and she managed to snag it before it hit the market.

The sound of crunching gravel brings my mind out of the past. A glint of sunlight reflects off a silver car traveling down one side of Gracewood Hall's two-lane driveway. Kate's head jerks in the direction of the approaching vehicle.

She stiffens and asks, "Are you expecting someone?"

Before I can answer, she sprints up the front steps and disappears inside.

What an odd reaction.

I watch the car as it draws closer. It's an older-model silver Honda Accord. I don't recognize it as a car driven by anyone I know. The sun reflects off the windshield, so I can't make out the driver. When the vehicle reaches the circle, it hugs the left as it travels around the fountain that adorns the center of the drive and slowly crawls toward the exit.

Gracewood Hall is an events venue. When the gates are open, as they are this morning, vendors, prospective clients, and the curious are constantly in and out.

Plus, the rehearsal dinner for the #Lo-An_wedding—as London has insisted we refer to all her wedding events—is this evening. So, a lot of people will be coming and going today. One of tonight's invited out-of-town guests might even have located the place early. As the car reaches the end of the driveway and turns right onto the road, a red Maserati spins in.

London has arrived. Anson is with her, no doubt. I realize I'm unsure what she has told her fiancé about her new maid of honor. I need to keep Kate tucked away until I know.

My job is a mix of service and discretion. By secreting Kate away for a while, I will avoid a potentially awkward situation for the bride.

Before the red car reaches the fountain, I duck inside and find Kate hidden around a corner, studying a painting on a wall in the room Gigi and I have named the parlor. It's off the grand foyer and can be closed off by gorgeous, carved wooden doors.

She startles when I enter the room and close the doors.

"Are you okay?" I ask.

"Of course," she says, but she eyes the door warily.

"Really? Are you sure? You seem a little spooked by that car. This place may seem like Highclere Castle, but it's an events venue. A lot of people come and go."

I'm sure she means her nod and shrug to convey nonchalance, but her stiff posture gives her away.

"Did the silver car stop?"

"No, it continued around the driveway and turned onto the highway. Kate, what's going on? Can you level with me and let me know if something is wrong? I have enough to worry about over the next two days."

Yikes. That sounds cold. But it's true.

She seems to shrink and bites her bottom lip. "I don't mean to add to your burden, Jenna, but lately, I've had the strangest feeling of being followed. That's one of the reasons

I was glad to get out of town. I think that silver Honda is the car that's been following me."

"Why would someone be following you?"

She shakes her head and shrugs.

"Have you told the police?"

She doesn't have time to answer before London's voice pierces the air. "I asked you to bring in the bag with my shoes, Anson. Go get it. Why don't you ever listen to me?"

Kate mouths, "The bride?"

I raise my brows and nod.

Confident that Anson will go out for the bag he forgot, I call, "Hi, London, we're in the parlor."

She opens the door, peers inside, then pauses on the threshold, looking skeptically from Kate to me and then back at Kate.

London's blonde hair is piled high in a messy bun. She's wearing a hot pink strapless romper that I suppose is fashionable but doesn't suit her. For the first time, I notice she has a tattoo below her collarbone. It says FIERCE in fancy script. Sometime between yesterday's debacle with Betsy and right now, she'd found the time to freshen up her spray tan because she's virtually glowing.

"This is Kate Asher," I say. "Kate, this is London Brinks. London, I wasn't sure what you told Anson about the maid of honor situation. Was Anson okay with Betsy not being in the wedding?"

London *tsks* and hitches her leather Prada bag onto her

bare shoulder.

"I did not give him a choice. I told him his sister was stressing me out, and I couldn't deal with her and the wedding, too."

"So, he understands that Betsy will not be in the wedding?"

London nods.

She's staring at Kate, who has pulled herself to her full height. Kate seems more like herself as she eyes London with an impassive expression.

They're like two dogs sizing each other up. I half-expect them to circle each other and start sniffing.

"As I said a moment ago," I say, "I wasn't sure how much you'd told Anson about Kate."

"I didn't tell him anything about Kate," London says irritably.

"Well, okay. That's fine, but you need to tell me how to proceed. You either know her and she was suddenly available to be in the wedding, or you need to tell your fiancé that you hired Kate to be your maid of honor. What do you want? I need to know so that I don't blow your cover."

"I didn't realize she was so … blonde." London bites her lower lip. "She won't look good in the shade of green I chose for the maid of honor's dress, but that's fine."

"I can wear an auburn wig if you'd like," Kate offers.

London's nostrils flare, and she gives a noncommittal one-shoulder tick.

I give London a palms-up shrug meant to convey the question, *what will it be?*

A moment later, her scowl transforms into a bright smile, and she closes the distance between her and Kate, pulling Kate into a hug. "Welcome to #Lo-An_wedding, bestie! I can't believe you could make it to the wedding," London gushes. "And you came all the way from Paris. Wait, I have something special for you."

Okay then. We're going for the lifelong best friend story. That's fine with me as long as I know so I can keep everything consistent.

London releases a bewildered-looking Kate, reaches into her purse, and pulls out a velvet pouch.

"I had this bracelet custom-made for my maid of honor to wear. Go ahead, put it on. You must wear it when you're out in public during the wedding weekend. I promised the jewelry designer it would be on full display in all the photos. So, make a point of showing it off."

Kate opens the pouch, pulls out the gold rope-style bangle, and slides it onto her slender wrist.

"It's lovely." She traces the pavé diamond-encrusted letters L and A, artfully woven together to look like a heart set into the bracelet's solid rope base. If you didn't know that the shape was made of two joined letters, you would likely think it was a fancy heart.

It's a little blingy for my taste, but it must be worth a small fortune with all the gold and diamonds.

The front door opens and slams shut. It's probably Anson.

"Kate and I are going to take a turn around the gardens and catch up." London laces her arm through Kate's and walks her faux bestie toward the doors leading outside.

She pauses at the door and calls over her shoulder, "Tell Anson to take my things upstairs and put them in the bride's room. Text me when the photographer gets here to do the pictures."

"Oh, Kate, how long has it been?" She lowers her voice. "Make sure I get that bracelet back at the end of the wedding."

Chapter Two

~ Maddie ~

"You are marrying *me*, idiot," London growls at Anson. "Eyes on me and off my best friend's cleavage."

Everyone freezes. Even the gentle spring breeze seems to hold its breath at the threat of London's brewing tantrum.

Foolishly, I'd hoped we could get through the rehearsal without drama. What was I thinking? I glance at my daughter, mentally telegraphing *how can I help*? Even though I know she can handle it.

"Why don't we take a break," she suggests.

I've never attended a wedding rehearsal where the bride and groom needed a break, but this isn't the average wedding.

Granted, my role is helping brides find the perfect dress. I'm not usually around for the wedding rehearsal or the wedding unless there's a need. However, since this is the inaugural event at Gracewood Hall, we decided an all-hands-on-deck approach would be best. The place is so large. The more staff we have on hand, the better to make sure the bride doesn't end up burning down the place or killing her groom.

"Anson, a word, please," London demands. "And you, Kate, cover up. Go put on a sweater or something."

The ceremony will take place outside under a tent, and the guests will move inside for the reception. It's too warm for a sweater, and there's nothing wrong with Kate's dress—unless Anson has X-ray vision.

A sullen London brushes past me with a cowed-looking Anson trailing behind her. They stop by the red oak tree about fifty feet away. I turn away because watching her tear into her fiancé is painful. I mean, I hadn't seen him staring at Kate's cleavage. Not that I'd been looking for it.

"Is this dress inappropriate?" Kate asks Jenna as they approach. "It's too warm to wear a turtleneck. Really, I don't think that would stop the groom. I've lost count of how often he's hit on me."

Oh. I stand corrected.

"Are you kidding?" I ask.

"No, I am not. I have never seen anything like this. I thought he was just a letch, but right before the rehearsal started, he cornered me and said he was trying to make London call it off. He said something about having contracts and losing money if he walked out."

Jenna rubs her temples. "Yes, they're social media influencers. They get paid to promote products and make it look like they have perfect lives. They'll be in breach of many contracts if this wedding isn't livestreamed tomorrow."

"But if he makes her mad enough to walk out, the wedding won't go on. Won't he lose out, too?"

"It all depends on what his contracts say." I lower my voice. "It's a strange arrangement getting married and having it livestreamed so that millions of people you've never met can see what you're doing and try to replicate it. Call me old-fashioned, but that's not what getting married is about. For all we know, as audacious as he's being, he might even have struck a deal to blow up everything."

"Well, that would explain why he's not even trying to be discreet, and London is getting upset with me over it." Kate rolls her eyes. "I'm afraid this marriage is in trouble before it begins. If London knew what was good for her, she would call off everything while she still can."

Jenna sighs. "Let's not speculate. I promised to give them a wedding, and I have to operate under the assumption that the groom is shaking out the last of his wild oats before he commits to forever. Our job is to steer him back onto the right path and ensure they get hitched without a hitch."

"Right, it wouldn't be a good look if the inaugural wedding at Gracewood Hall goes up in flames," Gigi says.

I hadn't realized she'd been standing behind us. We turn toward her.

"You know, there's a rumor that says the place is cursed," she says with a sparkle in her eyes.

Kate's brows lift. "Did you know that before you bought it?"

I hadn't heard that little nugget of lore about Gracewood Hall. I wouldn't put it past Gigi to have manufactured it. She loves making people wonder and speculate.

She's been away from Hemlock for years, living her own life. However, after Reggie Phillips, husband number four, passed away, leaving her a widow, she decided it was time to come home. Even though Gigi didn't marry her husbands for their money, each one had left her better off than the last. Between her cumulative inheritances, which she's wisely invested, and the $10 million she banked when she sold the Malibu, California, beachfront home she shared with Reggie, Gigi is a wealthy woman.

While she still believes in love, she maintains that she is not getting married a fifth time.

She loves to say, "I'm too old for a young man, but I'm too young at heart to tie myself down to some old codger with one foot in the grave."

"I want to be on my own for a while," she'd said. "I can't think of a better place to be than with my girls in Hemlock. You two are having so much fun, and I want some of what you're having. You own the bridal salon, and Jenna plans the events. All we're missing is the venue. Gracewood Hall will give us the trifecta."

Of course, I wonder if Gigi realized the hard work involved in actually getting *some of what we're having*.

Working with London straight out of the gate has been baptism by fire.

Gigi swats the air. "As intriguing as those rumors are, I believe they're a bunch of hogwash. But they do make people curious. Curiosity can lead to extra publicity. You know what they say, there's no such thing as bad publicity."

Jenna gives Gigi the side-eye. "I don't know about that, Geeg. Let's try to keep this wedding from turning into a dumpster fire. Okay? Is everyone on board?"

I nod, feeling bad for my daughter.

Gigi chuckles. "Of course, dear. Your Geeg is always on your side."

"Look, I'm sorry," Kate says. "I've worked dozens of weddings, and I can assure you the groom has never hit on me. This is a first. I'm here to help. I'll do whatever you need me to do."

"No worries," Jenna says. "We need to get back on schedule before people arrive for the rehearsal dinner. We need to wrap up the rehearsal in the next fifteen minutes so the bridal party will have time to get ready. Let me talk to London. I'll be right back."

"I'll go check on the dinner and make sure everything is on schedule," I offer.

"Thanks, Mom," Jenna says.

Walking toward the house, I notice that London and Anson are embracing. They seem to have made amends. They break apart when Jenna approaches and says something to them. Anson seizes the opportunity to get away. I see him beelining in Kate's direction.

"Okay, mister, I don't know what you're playing at," I murmur and turn around to head him off. "But you won't make this more difficult for us than you already have."

Jenna must also notice where Anson is heading. She sends London toward the house and jogs over to Kate.

As we converge on the groom and the maid of honor, a man I don't recognize walks up. He's probably about Jenna and Kate's age, and he's gorgeous. He has a chiseled face, dark brown hair, and startling blue eyes. The dark razor stubble on his cheeks and chin adds to his sultry, movie-star good looks.

"Kate, my love, there you are," he says.

"David?" Kate says.

"Who's David?" Anson asks.

Kate steps closer to David and puts her arm around him. "Darling, I'm so glad you're finally here."

"Yes, I was able to get away after all," David says.

Kate stares up at him adoringly. "I didn't have a doubt."

"Jenna, Maddie, this is David Martin, my boyfriend." Kate glances at Anson. "David, this is Anson Rutt, the groom."

David offers his hand. "Anson, it's nice to meet you. Did your lovely bride tell you that Kate was bringing someone to the wedding?"

There's an edge to David's voice, and I suspect he might

have witnessed London's most recent meltdown about Anson's wandering eye and is staking his claim.

Anson narrows his eyes at David and accepts the handshake.

"Nice to meet you, dude. London didn't tell me, but that doesn't mean anything. This is her gig. I'm sure it won't be a problem. Right, Jenna?"

A weighted silence hangs in the air.

I find it interesting that Kate, a professional bridesmaid who should be able to recite the principles of wedding etiquette by heart, would surprise the wedding planner with a plus-one the day before the wedding.

I would've thought Kate would want to focus solely on the bride and not have any distractions. Especially since the story goes that she and London are lifelong besties and Kate's schedule freed up at the last minute, allowing her to fly in from Paris for the wedding, but maybe Kate's boyfriend showing up makes the ruse seem more realistic.

Kate would want London to meet her boyfriend if they were best friends.

I don't know. I'm glad I do not have to worry about keeping everything straight. I feel bad that the weight is on my daughter's shoulders.

I figure the best thing I can do is to help her when she asks and stay out of the way the rest of the time.

"I'm sure it will work out," she says. "We always order extra meals."

My daughter's voice is tight, and she scribbles a note on the tablet she carries with her. The constant accessory has almost become an extension of her left hand.

There's an awkward beat of silence. Anson can't help himself and gives Kate one last once-over before shoving his hands in his pockets and inclining his head toward the minister. "I need to go talk to the preacher."

"Congratulations," David says. "I'm happy to be here to celebrate your big day."

"David Martin?" Jenna says after Anson is out of earshot. Her voice has more life to it now, as if she realizes that with David on the scene, Anson might mind his manners and suddenly only have eyes for his bride. "It's been a long time."

But there's still a note of worry in her voice. I suspect it will be there until London and Anson exchange vows and ride off into the moonlit night in the Bentley they've rented to take them to the Hemlock Inn, where they will spend their wedding night before getting up bright and early on Sunday morning and boarding a plane that will whisk them to a hotel that has agreed to foot the bill for an all-expense-paid honeymoon in Cabo San Lucas.

Most importantly, they will be out of our lives forever.

Shame on me. The most important thing is that London and Anson know a life of happiness … but I will be happy if they don't kill each other before the beef Wellington course at tomorrow night's reception.

"Yeah, Jenna, it's good to see you again," David says.

"The three of us went to college together," Jenna tells me. "I knew that they dated, but…" She turns back to the couple. "I thought you broke up." Jenna grimaces. "Sorry. Not to be indelicate."

"We did," Kate says, gazing up at David. "You know what they say about the course of true love—"

"It never did run smooth." David finishes her sentence. "But what matters is that we found our way back to each other, and here we are. Did Kate not tell you we're back in each other's lives?"

"It's been a bit of a whirlwind since she arrived this morning," Jenna says. "We haven't had a chance to catch up. But good for you two. I'm happy for you."

~ Jenna ~

I DIDN'T KNOW David very well in college. I only met him a couple of times. He and Kate hung out with a different group. I remember that they broke up about halfway through our senior year because Kate and I were partners on a project in one of our business classes, and she fell off the face of the earth for the crucial part of a week during that time. She resurfaced just in time to pull an all-nighter, during which she insisted on doing most of the work. We managed to snag an *A* on our project.

But after confessing that the breakup with David had

driven her to leave town, she had been strangely stoic, refusing to talk about it. It's interesting that they found their way back to each other.

Sometimes it takes going your separate ways and getting out in the real world to make you realize what you lost.

Under normal circumstances, I'd be over the moon for them, but Kate has been distracted since David arrived. I know how it is; I have a hard time focusing when I'm with my boyfriend, Ian, which is why he doesn't hang around the events I plan.

Plus, he's a lawyer and doesn't have much spare time for hanging.

After we'd herded all the cats back to the rehearsal, Kate almost blew her cover when she told London that she and David had met at the University of North Carolina. London had previously told Anson that Kate had attended the Sorbonne.

"Wait a minute," Anson said. "I thought she went to college in Paris."

"She did!" London had said.

"I did!" Kate had echoed.

"But you said you met that dude when you went to college in North Carolina," Anson had pressed.

London blinked and looked at Kate, clearly indicating that she was on her own explaining this one.

"I did some coursework at UNC," Kate had said without batting an eye. "A lot of people take classes at more than one higher learning institution."

Her tone implied that Anson was an idiot if he didn't know that.

Anson bit, saying, "I know."

He dropped the subject like a bad habit, finished the ceremony walkthrough, and everyone dispersed to their hotels.

Now, guests gather under the big white tent on Gracewood Hall's lawn for cocktails. We should be opening the doors to the dining room for the rehearsal dinner in twenty minutes. The bride and groom are here. So is Anson's brother, who is his best man, but I haven't seen Kate since she left to go back to her room at the Hemlock Inn to shower and change for the dinner.

Earlier, I texted her to let her know that London had decided she wanted Kate to give a toast at tonight's dinner—something sweet and nostalgic to drive home the fact that Kate *knew her when.*

London made me write it down. "Make sure she says, 'London told me I'm the only person she trusts because I knew her before she was rich and wildly Insta-famous.'"

It took everything I had to keep from rolling my eyes. Or gagging.

What stops me is that I feel bad for London because it's clear she desperately wants a lifelong best friend like the one she'd invented in Kate, but she manages to drive everyone away before the bond of friendship can set.

Right now, that's the least of my worries. Her imaginary

best friend is late.

Maybe Shakespeare should've reworded his famous *course of true love* saying to, the course of true love makes an otherwise intelligent businesswoman *lose her good sense.*

I walk over to a quiet corner of the dining room, which is bustling with waitstaff preparing for the intimate rehearsal dinner for two hundred and fifty—a rehearsal in its own right for tomorrow night's intimate soiree for five hundred— and take out my phone and type a message to Kate.

"I'm sorry about the last-minute rehearsal dinner toast. I hope it didn't throw you. I know it's unconventional, but what the bride wants… It's 6:45. Are you almost here? London wants to hear the toast before you give it."

Kate does one better than answer my text. She comes rushing into the dining room.

"Maddie told me you were in here. Sorry I'm cutting it so close."

She looks gorgeous in the shimmery gold cocktail dress she's wearing, and my first thought is, *Uh-oh. London will pitch a fit because Kate looks so good.*

For a moment, I rack my brain, trying to recall if there's something else in the bride's room Kate can change into if London objects too loudly. Then I decide that London needs to learn that she can't always be the prettiest woman in the room. In fact, it would behoove her to learn that women supporting other women will get her much further than constantly viewing other females as competition.

Or, at the very least, that substance over flash wins almost every time.

Or when it counts, anyway.

"No worries," I say as I lead her out of the dining room and into the parlor. "Is everything okay?"

Kate offers a one-shoulder shrug. That's when I notice that she looks more than frazzled.

"What's going on?"

She walks over to the window that looks out onto the front of the property.

"I saw that silver car again," she says. "It followed me here tonight."

"Did David drop you off? Did he see it, too?"

"No, he's catching up on some work. I drove myself."

"Are you sure it was the same one? Silver cars aren't exactly unique."

"It was the same one. It has a cracked headlight." Wringing her hands, she turns away from the window.

"Did you call the police?" I ask.

Kate shakes her head. "What would I say? I mean, is it illegal to follow someone? He or she—whoever is doing this—hasn't done or said anything to make me think they might hurt me. But it seems like every time I turn around, they're there. It's freaking me out."

"I'm not sure if it's illegal to follow someone, but if they're making you uncomfortable, it might be considered harassment. My mom is engaged to Hemlock's chief of police. I could ask him off the record. Do you have any idea who might be doing this?"

Kate shakes her head and inhales a slow, deep breath, letting it out at a measured pace.

"Have you had a disagreement with anyone? Maybe a disgruntled bride? Or did you date someone who might be upset that you and David are back together?"

"No. Not that I can think of. I'm sorry I'm freaking out like this. It's so unprofessional. Normally, I keep my personal life to myself when working, but this situation is not normal. Still, I apologize."

"No apology necessary," I say. "I'll call the chief and have him send someone to follow you home tonight. It will be late when we finish, and I don't want you to walk into the hotel alone."

"No, please don't. I will valet park when I get back to the hotel. Then I won't have to walk in from the parking lot."

"Okay, but please call David and have him meet you in the lobby. Deal?"

"Sure." Kate checks her posture, and I can virtually see her business mask slide into place. And just like that, she's the self-assured woman I've always known.

"Were you able to come up with a toast?" I ask. "I hated to ask that of you since it's so last minute. Especially when it's not customary for the maid of honor to give a toast at the rehearsal dinner. That's usually when other family members toast the bride and groom."

"I gave it my best shot," Kate says. "I hope London likes it."

"Don't shoot the messenger, but she wants to hear your toast before you give it."

"Okay, but if she doesn't like it, I can't guarantee that I can come up with anything better. Not at this late hour."

"I know, and I promise I'll be the go-between if she gets too unreasonable."

"If?" Kate asks. "Can that promise carry through tomorrow night?"

We look at each other and laugh.

"Let's get this over with," I say. "Why don't you go up to the office while I find London? It's the first door on the left at the top of the stairs. I'll send her up. By then, it will be time to start ushering people into the dining room. After she approves the toast, will you bring her downstairs, please?"

A barely there Mona Lisa smile tips up the edges of Kate's mouth. "Sure," she says. "We'll see you in a few minutes."

I start to go but turn back to her. "It's not a problem for David to come to the dinner tonight. Go ahead and call him if you'd like."

"Thanks, Jenna, but no. I'll see him later." This time, her mouth blooms into a full smile, and she seems like she's in love.

My faith in love and levelheaded businesswomen is restored.

Kate ascends the grand staircase, and I let myself out the back door and walk toward the cocktail tent. It sounds like a frat party.

"London, where are you?" calls a young woman who I hope is at least twenty-one because she grabs two shot glasses off the tray of a passing waiter and downs them successively. "London, you promised that we could get a picture together," she bellows again, even though London isn't nowhere near her.

I notice that she is wearing a hot-pink wristband that says she showed proof of legal drinking age when she checked in. The events staff was under strict orders to apply the wristbands tightly enough that they could not be slipped off and shared. Under no circumstances were they to let a guest who wanted to imbibe walk away with a wristband in hand. As long as they stick to the rules, my company, Champagne Wedding and Event Designs, and Gracewood Hall won't be liable for contributing to the delinquency of a minor.

"Do you know where London is?" I ask her.

"*Nooo*, and she promised we could get a picture together."

She sets the empty shot glasses on the tray of another passing server and grabs two more shots.

"Easy there," I say. "It's still early. You might want to pace yourself."

The woman slurs something that sounds dangerously

close to, "Dude, hop off."

As I signal the bartender to cut her off, my phone dings a text message. It's from my mom. *"London needs to see you. She's in the office and is upset because she doesn't like Kate's toast. Kate says it's too late to change it. You should know, when I asked London how much she'd had to drink, she said she was on her second bottle of Veuve."*

I answer, *"Thanks for letting me know. Ask Kate to help you keep London in the office. If you can, make some coffee. We need to sober her up before she makes her entrance tonight."*

Speaking of people who need to be handled … where is Anson?

I glance around and finally spy the groom with a cute blonde in the cocktail tent. They're playing the drinking game quarters with tequila snake bites. Every time one of them takes a shot, the crowd cheers.

It's not ideal that the groom will be wasted, but I need to choose my battles, and right now, the angry bride takes precedence.

I trot toward the house, dodging people and trying not to let my heels get stuck in the grass. I text Gigi and ask her to tell Tess Harrison, whose company, Briar Patch Catering, is providing the food for the #Lo-An_wedding extravaganza, to keep the dining room doors shut until we give the okay to let people in.

She texts back, *"Gotcha covered."*

I've just let myself in the back door when London's unmistakable shriek pierces the air. An eerie silence falls over the place, then chaos ensues.

"She's not breathing!" London cries.

"I think she's dead," someone says.

"Someone call 911!" a woman demands.

I push through the people crowded in front of the ladies' room at the end of the hall behind the grand staircase.

"Move back, everyone," I insist. "Move back now."

As the sea of people parts, I see London, looking ghostly pale, standing over Kate's motionless body and clutching a champagne bottle.

An expanding maroon halo blooms on the terrazzo floor beneath Kate's head.

Chapter Three

~ *Maddie* ~

THE MOST CHALLENGING part of owning a bridal shop is helping brides balance the big opinions of friends and family with her vision of her dream dress. It's not easy.

Sometimes when there's a large entourage and certain individuals forget that it's the bride's choice, that they've been invited to *ooh* and *ahh* and lend support, it can devolve into tears and cross words.

It's not fun, but at least a murder has never taken place in my shop.

The paramedics have pronounced Kate dead by the time Jackson Bradley, Hemlock's chief of police, arrives on the scene. I'm standing about ten yards away, but I see them covering her with a white sheet.

"Did you or anyone else see what happened?" the chief asks me.

I watch Tess and her staff assist the police in corralling the rehearsal dinner guests in the dining room for questioning. As she tries to shut one of the doors, people crane their necks to see the dead body.

I shudder and bring Chief Bradley up to speed on everything I know that transpired before London's scream alerted us that something was wrong.

"One moment Kate was in the office quarreling with London Brinks over the toast that she wanted Kate to give at tonight's dinner—"

"Kate is the deceased?" Jack confirms.

I nod.

"What's her last name?"

"Asher. Kate Asher."

"Who is London Brinks?" Jack glances up at me from the notebook in which he'd been writing, pen poised in midair.

Who is London? Now, that's a loaded question. Where do I even begin?

"London Brinks is the bride," I say. "This weekend, Jenna, Gigi, and I were facilitating her wedding to Anson Rutt at Gracewood Hall. Tonight was supposed to be the rehearsal dinner. The rehearsal was earlier, and the wedding was supposed to be tomorrow.

"London had asked Kate to write a toast to give at the dinner tonight, but when London read it, she didn't like it and wanted Kate to redo it. Kate told her she wouldn't. She said London hadn't given her enough notice, that it was this speech or nothing.

"Then London said, 'I will literally kill you if you give that toast.'" I cringe at how damming it sounds. "Jack, I don't think she meant it. She was about halfway through her second bottle of champagne, and she was a little intoxicated." I realize that piece of the puzzle probably didn't help things, but I had to tell him.

"Those were her exact words?" Jack says.

I squeeze my eyes shut and nod. When I open them, Jack is still writing in his notebook.

"I tried to defuse the situation by telling London that it wasn't customary for the maid of honor to give a toast at the rehearsal dinner. I suggested we scrap tonight's toast, put our heads together, and figure out a special one for tomorrow night's reception. London insisted that she wanted two speeches. Kate told her if she wanted two, London needed to write one herself or be happy with the one Kate had proposed."

"How long have these two known each other?" Jack says.

I explain the bridesmaid-for-hire situation and how Kate hires herself out to brides in need. "London said she was upset because Kate was supposed to make her happy, not stir things up. Then she accused Kate of running a shoddy business. I could tell Kate was offended. Because when she left the room, she said, 'I'm going to the ladies' room. I will talk to you when you can treat me with respect.'

"Kate left. London sat here for a minute, complaining that Kate wasn't allowed to walk away from her and saying she wouldn't pay her.

"Then London left the room. I could hear her yelling

down the stairs, 'Do not walk away from me when I'm talking to you. I am paying you to be at my beck and call this weekend. Basically, I own you. Get back here and come up with a decent toast.'

"It was quiet for a moment, and then I heard London scream."

"Did you hear Kate scream, or was there any noise that would've indicated a struggle?" Jack says.

I shake my head and tears sting my eyes. "A woman is dead at the opening of Gracewood Hall. We brought Kate here."

"I'm sorry," the chief says. "Are you okay?" He tilts up my chin with his finger and looks into my eyes.

Did I mention that Jack and I are engaged?

We met when I called the police station with a procedural question for the Aubrey Christensen cozy mystery series I write. He was so helpful and generous with his time, I insisted on repaying him with coffee. Of course, I had an ulterior motive. Once a writer discovers a great source, keeping them properly fed and watered pays off.

That thank-you coffee led to us meeting at the Briar Patch most mornings. Before I opened the bridal shop, I'd go to the bakery and write my requisite two pages. Like clockwork, Jack would show up as I powered down my laptop. We'd shoot the breeze until we had to go to work. As the months went on, pulling ourselves away became harder and harder.

We had chemistry. At first, everyone but us could see it.

But things were complicated.

He was a widower who hadn't come to terms with the loss of his wife, and my predicament was that I didn't know whether Frank, my navy pilot husband, who had been missing in the line of duty for years, was alive or dead.

I couldn't give up on Frank because once I stopped believing he was alive, it meant he was … gone. Until the day the navy knocked on my door with the official news, I couldn't give up on him.

Or admit to myself that I was interested in anyone other than my first and only love.

Eventually, that fateful day happened.

Now, here we are. Jack and I are getting married. If I can get the nerve to set a date.

However, that's a minor problem compared to Kate being murdered at Gracewood Hall.

"I'm fine," I say. "Or at least I will be once you catch the person who did this to Kate."

"My wedding is ruined." The sound of London's hysterical sobs causes Jack and me to flinch apart. "I was supposed to livestream tonight. What am I supposed to do now?"

Jack's right brow shoots up, and he looks from me to his deputy, Jeff Salisbury, who is escorting an agitated London out of the dining room.

She looks a mess. Her hair is mussed, her makeup is more off than on, and mascara runs in black rivers down her cheeks.

She jerks her arm out of Jeff's grasp and goes still, staring at Kate's sheet-covered body. I watch all the color drain from her freshly spray-tanned face.

I think she's in shock.

Then again, I remember how mercurial and impulsive she can be.

Maybe seeing the results of her actions is hitting home.

Did London lash out at Kate over the toast? Did London hit her or accidentally push her, causing Kate to lose her balance and whack her head on the terrazzo floor, or whatever caused Kate's head to split open and spill blood all over the place?

I blink away the thought. As damning as it looks, there's no proof that London attacked Kate. Not only is London innocent until proven guilty, but she shouldn't even be considered a suspect until Jack has gathered enough evidence.

That said, I will not speculate or ponder anything beyond what I know to be the absolute truth.

However, if London keeps whining about how Kate ruined the wedding, she might incriminate herself.

As I watch London finally acquiesce and let Jeff lead her away from the body, the reality of the situation comes crashing down—Jenna's friend, Kate Asher, is dead. She might still be alive if she hadn't been called in for this shambled wedding spectacle. How did we even get caught in this mess?

A sob escapes my throat before I can stop it.

"Hey, are you okay?" Jack puts a steadying hand on my shoulder. "Why don't we go into one of the offices? You can sit down and maybe have a glass of water."

"We can use Jenna's office because I do need to sit. Where is Jenna, by the way? Have you seen her? She must be so upset. Kate was a college friend of hers."

Jack's brow goes up again, and I remember a time when Jenna's ex-boyfriend, Riley Buxston, had been murdered, and for the blink of an eye, my daughter had been implicated.

"Jenna did not do this," I say through gritted teeth. "We are not going through that again, are we?"

Jack lets out a heavy breath. "Jenna is talking to Steve Bledsoe. I'm sure he'll clear her."

The irrational thought of arguing with Jack grips me like two hands squeezing the life out of my throat, which makes it difficult to talk. Thank goodness, because I want to shout at Jack and tell him that there's nothing from which my daughter needs to be cleared.

Silently, I follow Jack up the grand staircase to Jenna's office. When he opens the door, I see that my daughter is in there with the officer, just as Jack said. She's been crying and looks as anguished as I feared she would, but seeing her is like a touchstone that grounds me and makes me feel better.

She stands up and runs to me. I pull her into a mama-bear hug. She's twenty-seven years old. I don't care how old she is, I will always become a mama bear if there's any chance she's in danger.

Danger.

The thought makes my stomach plummet. The farfetched chance that she would be implicated in Kate's death pales in comparison to the reality that someone did kill Kate. The killer is on the loose—or maybe in the dining room.

Until the police apprehend the murderer, we are all in danger.

"Mom?" Jenna squeaks. "Who would do this to Kate?"

I shake my head, and Jack puts a hand on my shoulder.

"Look, you and I need to leave Steve and Jenna to their conversation and go somewhere else."

I'm glad he said conversation and not questioning.

Because Jenna needed to tell the authorities everything she knew. It didn't mean that they suspected her as they did when Riley Buxston died.

I squeeze Jenna's hand. She squeezes mine back.

Jack and I step out into the hall.

"We could go into the bride's room," I suggest.

"It's already been cordoned off and is being searched."

He points to two winged-back chairs with a small, wooden round table between them positioned by the window.

When we're seated, he gives me a moment to collect myself. In the distance, I can hear the faint murmur of voices from downstairs.

"How can you be sure you've detained everyone?" I ask. "What if the killer got away?"

"I will need to see a guest list," he says. "Were the same people invited to the wedding tomorrow?"

"Yes, but not everyone attending the wedding was invited to the dinner tonight," I say.

"How many are here tonight?" he asks.

"Two-hundred and fifty were invited tonight."

Jack looks up and squints at me. "Two hundred and fifty people were coming to dinner?"

I nod.

"How many are invited to the wedding?"

"Five hundred."

His mouth falls open. "I don't even know two hundred and fifty people, much less that many I would want to attend our wedding. That's not the kind of wedding you want, is it?" He holds up his hand and stops me before I can answer. "Let's talk about that later."

"For the record, no. I don't want a big fancy affair. We'll talk about it later."

He looks relieved. We've been engaged for a while and haven't set a date yet, but it's good to know the parameters.

"So, five hundred people were invited," he says. "Surely, not all of them are coming."

"Oh, yes, they are. The Hemlock Inn is booked solid. Some guests are local, and others are driving in from out of town."

"So, the bride is from Hemlock?" He pages back and looks at his notes. "I don't know a London Brinks or an Anson Rutt."

"Of course, you don't. London is from Los Angeles by way of Georgia."

I start from the beginning and tell him about London and her wedding, which was supposed to put Hemlock and Gracewood Hall on the map, but in the shadow of Kate's death, that seems trivial now.

When I finish bringing Jack up to speed, he closes his notebook and scratches his head. He looks confused. Or maybe perplexed is a better word for it.

"I know," I say. "The entire experience of facilitating a social media influencer's wedding has been just this side of surreal. Things have been anything but perfect in real life. But we are supposed to make everything appear *Insta* perfect."

"What?" Jack says.

"For Instagram. You know, social media."

He frowns. "Okay. And you say the bride, this London…" He thumbs back through his notebook. "Brinks. London Brinks. Has been difficult to deal with?"

"Putting it mildly. Look, Jack, talking about a client this way makes me uncomfortable." I shrug. "I'm not sure how else to accurately portray the situation."

"Answer the questions truthfully. That's all you can do.

So, the deceased was a bridesmaid for hire. Are you aware of any prior history between Kate and the bride? I mean before London hired her."

"No. As far as I know, they met for the first time this morning. Jenna knows Kate from college and hired her after London kicked each person in her bridal party out of the wedding. She hired Kate as a last resort."

"You said the bride and the deceased exchanged words moments before the victim's body was discovered?"

I nod and repeat what I've already said about the toast. "To be honest, London was pretty rude about it. Of course, by that time, London was well into her second bottle of champagne. She called Kate names that were a bit ... colorful. Kate told London she would talk to her after she calmed down and they could have a respectful conversation. And Kate walked away."

"What did she do after Kate walked away?"

I study my hands and weigh my words, trying to decide the best way to say this next part.

"Maddie?" Jack says gently. "What did London do?"

"She went after Kate."

"And the bride was the one found with the body?" Jack says.

I nod and swallow a wave of nausea. This is not looking good for London.

"How much time passed between London going after Kate and her discovering the body?"

I shrug again. "Minutes? Not very long."

"Thanks, Maddie. I think we're done here." He leans in and takes my hand. "I'm so sorry this has happened."

He stands, but I need to sit a moment. I'm feeling a little shaky.

Jack looks back at me. "You okay?"

I nod.

"Listen, I know I don't have to tell you this," he says, "but stick around. Okay?"

~ *Jenna* ~

"I DID NOT kill Kate Asher," London hisses. "I just met her today. I don't even know her."

Jack is interviewing London in my office. I'm watching from the doorway. I'm probably not supposed to be there, but the door is open. I'm trying to make myself as inconspicuous as possible.

"You don't know Kate Asher?" Jack sounds incredulous. "But she was your maid of honor. How can you not know her?"

I know Jack has already gotten the full story from my mom when he questioned her. So, I'm sure he's pretending not to know to make sure London's story matches Mom's.

"It's a long story." London huffs and crosses her arms over her chest. "Am I under arrest? Because if I'm not, I would like to leave."

She stands up.

"You're not under arrest, but I do want to ask you some questions since you were the last one to see Kate Asher before you found her dead," Jack says. "We can do this the easy way or the hard way. It's up to you."

London sits down.

I know Jack means that if she doesn't cooperate, he will move this party to the police station. I'm hoping London doesn't test him because he doesn't care how many social media followers she has. Chief Jackson Bradley doesn't play.

"There were people in the dining room," London says. "And right next to where I found her body, there is an exit. Anyone could've come and gone through it before I got there. If you were doing your job rather than harassing me, you would already know that."

"Did you see anyone enter or exit through that door, Ms. Brinks?"

London's face scrunches into an irritable mask. "This is my wedding weekend. How dare you ruin it for me. You should be ashamed of yourselves. For that matter, I will not say another word until my lawyer gets here. That might be a while since he's coming from California."

She draws her fingers across her lips and then crosses her arms.

"Okay, I'll note that the witness is uncooperative, but I will wait until your attorney arrives. It is your right."

London spies me standing there.

"Jenna, you have to help me. This person… This…" She slants a distasteful look at Jack. "This police officer is keeping me away from my party."

I blink at her, astounded that she can even think about a party after all that's happened. However, I am the wedding planner. It is my job to take care of the details.

"London, as you can imagine," I say in the most soothing voice I can muster, "we've had to cancel the party."

"What did you tell everyone?" she demands. "We were supposed to livestream. It can't get out that someone was murdered at my rehearsal dinner."

"Livestream?" Jack says. "Were your cameras set up? Were they recording at the time of the murder?"

London scowls at Jack. "I told you I'm not talking to you until my lawyer arrives."

"That's too bad because if we had footage showing who killed Kate Asher, it might exonerate you. But we can play it your way. We can wait right here until your lawyer gets here. Or better yet, would you like to give your statement at the police station? I have a patrol car parked outside the house. I'm happy to give you a ride."

London rolls her eyes. "Kate was killed outside the bathroom," she says. "Why would I livestream in front of the bathroom? That's ridiculous." She rolls her eyes again, and the room falls silent.

"Speaking of footage," Jack says. "Jenna, since you're

lurking in the doorway, you might as well make yourself useful. Has Gigi installed security cameras inside or around the place?"

My heart sinks. If only.

"Not yet. The security company had to order the cameras, and the equipment won't arrive until next week."

"That's too bad," Jack says. I'm waiting for him to close the door or ask me to leave, but to my surprise, he doesn't. He turns his attention back to London and peppers her with questions.

A moment later, I startle at the touch of someone's hand on my shoulder.

I whirl around. My boyfriend, Ian McCoy, is standing there, looking as handsome as ever in a gray suit, white button-down, and green tie that matches the sea glass color of his eyes. He's holding a briefcase.

"Hi," I say. "What are you doing here?"

"The firm was asked to represent London Brinks," he says. "Her attorney is in Los Angeles and can't get here until Monday. Since I'm in Hemlock. Tag. I'm it."

Ian is a criminal lawyer and a darned good one. London will be lucky to have him on her side, though I feel bad for Ian having to babysit her through the weekend.

After I tell Ian everything I know, he enters the room. "Hello, Chief," he says to Jack. "I need to speak with Ms. Brinks."

"Who are you?" London's eyes brighten and take on a

greedy look as her gaze rakes up and down Ian's body. He's a good-looking man. I'm not surprised by her reaction.

"Ms. Brinks, I'm Ian McCoy from the Stanley, Howard, and Cash law firm in Asheville.

"You're representing Ms. Brinks?" Jack says.

"I will be after we formalize things," Ian says. "Your attorney, Clint Evans, from Evans and Reid in Los Angeles, contacted me. He asked me to fill in for him until he gets here. Would you like me to represent you until he arrives, Ms. Brinks?"

"Do you know this guy?" London asks me. "I saw you talking to him out there."

"I do. He's a good lawyer."

London dips her head, peers up at Ian through her lashes, and nods.

"Alright then," Ian says. "Chief, is my client under arrest?"

"No." There's a note in Jack's voice that implies *not yet*.

"In that case, please give us a few moments alone so she can bring me up to speed?"

"Of course," Jack says. "But don't take all night."

"I want Jenna to be in here," London insists as Jack leaves the room. She looks at Ian.

"This guy smells like expensive cologne and bad decisions," she says. "I need her here to keep me honest."

Is she serious right now? The police are questioning her because she found a dead body and she's flirting. Lovely.

Of course, I'll stay. I'd like to hear London's version of the story when the cops aren't in the room.

"Jenna, do you mind?" Ian asks.

"I'm happy to help in any way I can," I say as I enter the room and sit in the chair across from my desk, though I don't know what I can do except be there for moral support and maybe fetch coffee or water.

I'm about to offer that when Ian says, "Let's get the unpleasant part over with straight away. Ms. Brinks, did you kill Kate Asher?"

London's mouth falls open, and she glares at Ian as if he's suggesting something obscene. I suppose, by asking if she was a murderer, he has.

"Go away," she says, shooing him like he's a foul odor. "I thought I liked you, especially since Clint recommended you, but now I don't. Goodbye. Shoo. Go."

She crosses her arms and takes on the same stony demeanor she took with Jack.

"I'm not accusing you, Ms. Brinks," he says. "It's a standard question I have to ask. A simple yes or no answer will do, and then we can move on."

"I thought you said this guy was a good lawyer, Jenna." London's lip is curled back so far I can see her gums.

"He is good, London." I take care to keep my voice neutral. "You are lucky Ian has agreed to step in until your attorney can get here. Just answer the question, please."

"I. Did. Not. Kill. Kate. Asher." She bites off the words

and spits out each one like pieces of rotten meat.

"Okay," Ian says. "Good to know. Now let's talk about why the police chief thinks he has reason to detain you."

"I have no idea what he's thinking. What part of *I didn't do it*, don't you understand? This is my wedding weekend. I'm supposed to be live broadcasting the events on all my channels. Now, everything is ruined. What am I supposed to tell my followers?"

As Ian low-key questions London's values without exactly calling her a horrible human being, her words trigger something in my subconscious.

What am I supposed to tell my followers?
Followers…

"Oh, my gosh! Because of everything that's happened tonight, it completely slipped my mind that Kate told me she thought she was being followed."

Chapter Four

~ Maddie ~

IN ADDITION TO owning and running Blissful Beginnings Bridal Boutique, I also write cozy mysteries. I've been at it for several years. When I finally got my lucky break last year, I sold the five books I'd written in my Aubry Christensen mystery series. I've recently contracted for two more books.

After the joy of my dream coming true wore off, I was left with the abject horror of not only having to write two more good books that would keep the readers enthralled—but this time, I'd have to do it on deadline.

No pressure.

Giving myself credit, I've already developed the daily habit of writing two pages every morning. Now, because I've fallen so far behind, I have to up that to four pages a day, but I can do it since I know what's at stake.

The nice thing is that Jack meets me there most mornings, and we talk about life and police procedural tidbits for my stories. It's nice being engaged to my expert source.

However, being the police chief comes with certain responsibilities, such as not discussing active investigations. He tries to be firm, but we've learned to work around certain sticky issues. For example, when there's an active investigation and I want to ask questions, I pose the questions hypothetically.

That's what I do as I ride with Jack to the Hemlock Inn to break the news about Kate's death to her boyfriend, David.

"Hypothetically, would you arrest someone who was caught standing over the body of the deceased if she—or he—because we are talking hypothetically, of course—but if investigators determined that the victim died of—oh, let's say hypothetically ... blunt force trauma and the woman—or man—who found the body had been seen with a bottle—err, uhh ... hammer—the object that fits the profile of the murder weapon ... would you arrest her? Or him?"

"Maddie, don't, okay?" Jack rubs his eyes. "Not now, okay?"

We drive in silence.

After a while, Jack asks me, "Jenna knows David Martin from college?"

I'm tempted to say, *I thought you didn't want to discuss it*, but I don't.

"Yes, she said David and Kate dated in college, broke up for a while, and recently got back together."

I tell Jack how David surprised Kate by showing up at Gracewood Hall.

"Thank you," he says. "I'm sorry. I don't mean to be so gruff. I'm stressed. To answer your question, I didn't have enough evidence to hold London. I need to wait for some evidence we gathered tonight to come back from the lab. In the meantime, I released her on the condition that she sticks around in case we need to talk to her."

London has such a social media presence it wouldn't be difficult to find her.

I know that one of the pieces of evidence is the dress that London was wearing tonight. She was furious that she had to hand it over. But based on what I know, the lab will test it for Kate's blood. If London was the one who hit or pushed Kate, the dress will show evidence of blood spatter.

Also, London was holding an open half-full bottle of champagne. If she clubbed Kate over the head with it, there will be evidence of the champagne spilling down the arm of her dominant hand as she raised the bottle to hit Kate.

However, if London's story that she dropped the champagne bottle when she discovered Kate's body is true, then the lab will report that the champagne and tiny glass fragments sprayed the skirt of London's maxi dress accordingly.

The bottom line is if she is innocent, this lab report will exonerate her.

"I don't think London killed Kate," I say, hoping Jack will open up. "But the question remains, who did?"

Jack grunts an evasive answer.

"Are you okay?" I ask.

He slants a glance at me. "Yeah, I'm tired."

I don't press him since he doesn't want to talk.

Instead, I take out my phone and send a group text to Gigi and Jenna with the offer to stay at my place tonight and for as long as they want since a murder happened on the main floor of their new homes.

As I press send, my phone sounds the arrival of an incoming text.

It's from my assistant, Iris Hanson. Iris is a junior at Hemlock College. After my books sold, I thought hiring an assistant to handle some of the non-writing things that can be such time bandits would be helpful. Iris handles my social media, proofs my pages, and does other less glamorous things such as walking my two corgis, Agatha Christie and Sherlock Holmes. Aggie and Homie for short.

"Checking in to let you know Aggie and Homie have been fed, watered, and walked. Do you need me to do anything else?"

I type back, *"Thanks so much, Iris. That should do it. It's nearly 10:00. Please go home and enjoy your weekend."*

Of course, there's a killer on the loose, and the mother hen in me wants to warn her, but the murder hasn't been officially announced yet.

So, I add, *"And please be safe!"*

I watch the three little dots dance as Iris replies.

"But you have the wedding tomorrow. Don't you need me to take care of the corgis?"

Oh, that's right.

"There's been a slight change of plans. I should be able to take care of them tomorrow. I'll see you Monday."

"Okay, let me know if anything changes. Oh, and I read the chapter you sent me. So. Good. I'm dying to know what happens next! Please send more pages."

"What are you smiling about?" Jack says as he steers the car into the Hemlock Inn's parking lot.

"I got a text from Iris that she's taking good care of the dogs. And she happens to love the new chapter I asked her to proof."

"Well, I happen to love your smile." He leans in and kisses me, lingering with his forehead on mine. "So, save it for me while I go inside. I'll be back as soon as I can. Are you staying in the car?"

"I don't know. I might go in and sit at a table in the restaurant and write."

And while I'm there, I could question Natasha Merrell, the bar manager at Hemingways, the restaurant inside the Hemlock Inn. Of course, I don't tell Jack because he will tell me not to talk to Natasha about the case.

"Okay, well, I might be a while. I'm going up to Kate's room to talk to David." He hesitates, and I know even before he says a word that he hates this part of the job. "It's never easy to break news like this to loved ones."

"Do you want me to go with you?"

My heart hurts for David. The sudden and unexpected death of a loved one is traumatic. He and Kate had found each other again. They seemed so happy, as if their future was stretched out in front of them like an endless, meandering road with unexpected twists and turns.

I'm sure they never thought any roads would lead to this. Especially after finding each other again after all these years.

You never know what tomorrow holds.

"I appreciate the offer," Jack says, "but this is official business. Even though she wasn't killed at the inn, her room could hold clues."

I nod and realize that while I would go if Jack needed me to, I really don't want to be there when David gets the bad news.

It's one of the worst days of your life.

My late husband, Frank, was missing in action for years before the navy chaplain showed up at my front door with the news that I had both dreaded and didn't believe would ever come. Frank was the reason my life stood still for nearly a decade. I couldn't move forward without him because that would mean I'd given up on him. It would've meant he was really and truly gone if I gave up.

Now, I know Frank is really and truly gone.

My heart hurts, and the overwhelming urge to cry scalds the back of my throat.

Jack wants to set a date for our wedding, but I keep putting it off for various reasons.

After the Gracewood Hall renovations are completed, we could get married there.

After London's big wedding at Gracewood Hall.
After I finish this book.
Tomorrow.

I read something recently that says there's no such thing as tomorrow. All we have is the moment in which we're living.

Right now.

It's been fifteen months since Jack proposed that morning at the Briar Patch with family and friends around us. All the previous barriers that supposedly stood in the way of us setting a date are gone. I don't fully understand why the prospect of committing freaks me out. I don't want to lose Jack, but all I know is I freeze when I think of making our relationship officially official.

"Lock the doors," Jack says.

As he's getting out of the car, I stop him with a hand on his back. He turns to me. I lean in and kiss him. That old familiar push-pull of *what would I do without him, but am I really ready to live with someone else after being on my own for all these years* plays tug-of-war with my heart.

"I love you," I say.

"Love you, too."

He disappears through the inn's rotating brass front door. Through the picture window, I watch him approach the desk and speak to Sabrina Parsons, the manager of the Hemlock Inn.

Her eyes widen, and I know that Jack has broken the

news about Kate. After a brief exchange, Sabrina disappears into the office behind the front desk.

I'll sit here until Jack goes up to Kate's room. That way, if I do want to ask Natasha questions, he won't tell me I can't. He has an uncanny way of reading my mind—like a sixth sense—when I'm about to do something he'd prefer I not do.

That's another thing that annoys me. Since we've gotten engaged, Jack has seemed more controlling. Not in an abusive way, but more like *move over; I have a job to do, and you're in my way*. It hasn't always been like this. Not with Jack, anyway.

Frank … he was a loving husband, but he'd also been bossy. He was in the military and was used to barking orders and watching his subordinates hop to.

He and I got married when we were eighteen. We were newlyweds. I was so young and in love that it never occurred to me to be offended by his domineering ways. A year later, we had Jenna. By that time, Frank was advancing in his career. Pretty soon, he was away more than he was at home. When he was home, I always wanted to make the experience warm and welcoming for him.

I'm older now. I've been on my own for a long time.

Sometimes, I wonder if I'm cut out for living with someone twenty-four-seven.

Or maybe it's pre-wedding jitters.

Jack is a good guy. Why am I such a mess?

Rather than letting my monkey mind get the best of me while I wait for Jack to go upstairs, I open my notebook and try to focus on the story I'm writing.

Writing in a notebook is not the most efficient way to write a book, but it's better than sitting here doing nothing in cases like this. Plus, when I'm not in the mood to write, or I'm stuck in a scene, putting pencil to paper breaks down the wall between the story and me.

I scribble a sentence on the page, then line through it and stare at the rejected words, trying to figure out what's wrong with them.

They're … not right.

That's the story of my life lately.

That's why I need to grab every spare moment to make progress on the book. All I need to do is come up with the next sentence… But even after I push aside my wedding date problem, my brain fixates on what happened tonight. All I can see in my mind's eye is Kate lying motionless in a pool of blood.

Not to be insensitive to the fact that a young woman is dead, but murder was not what we'd planned for the big launch of Gracewood Hall as a wedding venue. Now, it feels haunted. If not literally, figuratively.

I'm already bracing myself for the days ahead and thinking about how we should handle the fallout. Underneath the lined-out first sentence of my chapter, I write, M*EET WITH* G*IGI AND* J*ENNA TO DEVELOP A CRISIS PUBLIC RELATIONS*

PLAN.

It feels selfish to think about the consequences we might face when Kate and David have lost so much more than we have over this unfortunate turn of events.

I'm staring into the middle distance of the lobby, trying to form the right words for the book, when Sabrina returns to the front desk. She taps on the computer, writes something on a piece of paper, and hands it to Jack.

She's given him Kate's room number, no doubt. Maybe even a key.

He walks toward the elevators, probably going up to Kate's room, where he will break the news to David and then look around.

Is it safe for him to go up there alone?

What if the killer has the same idea about accessing Kate's room?

Jack has his portable radio, but that's a far cry from officers backing him up. But the rest of the small Hemlock police force is still interviewing rehearsal dinner guests at Gracewood Hall, fifteen minutes away.

Should I go up there just in case? He'll be furious with me, but better mad than dead.

Chewing on the end of my pen, I glance around and try to gather my thoughts.

Yes, definitely better mad than dead.

I tuck my pen and notebook into my bag. As I get out of the car, I spy a silver Honda backed into a parking space in the single row of guest parking spots directly across from where we're parked.

One of the headlights is cracked. Like the car that Jenna told me had been following Kate.

My heart nearly stops.

Is this the car that was following Kate? She'd said she'd seen it parked outside the inn as she'd left to return to Gracewood Hall for the rehearsal.

I know Jack had planned to look at surveillance video footage to see if the security cameras had recorded a silver Honda or, better yet, the driver.

I take out my phone and start texting Jack about the car, but I stop. It will be a while before he can come down.

A streetlight shines on the car, and I can see through the windshield. No one is sitting behind the wheel.

That's good. It means it will be here for a while.

But what if the driver returns before Jack can get down here?

What if the car is outside the security camera's angle? I glance around, trying to find the equipment, but I don't see it.

If I text Jack about the car, he will tell me to sit tight and leave it alone.

Of course, he would probably call for another unit to come by and check it out, but that will take too long.

I hurry over to the Honda. A row of hedges runs along the back of the parking spaces, separating it from the road.

Since the car is backed in, there's not much room between its bumper and the hedgerow.

Still, I wedge my way in, hold my phone down, and snap several shots of the license tag.

I'm scrolling through to ensure I've got a clear photo of the license tag number when a man asks, "May I help you?"

Gasping, I see a tall, beefy, bald guy with a gray handlebar mustache approaching the Honda.

He's frowning at me.

When I say nothing, he asks, "What are you doing?"

My mind goes blank as I sidestep from the bushes, away from the car.

His gaze drops to the phone in my hands.

"My phone," I murmur. "I was getting out of my car and dropped my phone. It slid … back there."

I gesture to the trunk of his car with my phone.

His gaze slides to where I'd been standing when he surprised me. Since his attention is trained elsewhere, I switch my phone from the photo gallery back to the camera and stealthily—or at least I hope I'm being discreet—snap a photo of him and the car.

He eyes the car parked next to his—the one I'd said I was getting out of when I dropped my phone.

"That your car?" he asks.

I nod.

"So, why are you standing here? Why aren't you getting in it?"

I don't like his attitude.

Why were you following Kate?

Did you kill her?

If he did, why was he back here? He didn't seem spooked by the parked patrol car. Even so, it was almost like he was returning to the scene of the crime ... despite the technicality that Kate wasn't murdered here.

But she was murdered, and she had been staying at the Hemlock Inn.

And just like that, I realize this man very well might be Kate's killer. With the hedge behind me, the cars beside me, and him standing between me and the inn, he pretty much has me hemmed in.

Rather than cower, I muster all the annoyance I can convey and snap, "Because I'm not leaving. I'm going inside. To meet my fiancé, who is waiting for me."

I almost add *my fiancé, the chief of police. That's his car right over there. Would you like to meet him?*

But I bite back the words before they can escape. I don't want to drive the guy away, and if he's guilty of following Kate or killing her, that will surely do it. Or he might even start following me—or the unfortunate person who owns the car parked next to his. He might try to follow them, thinking it's me.

I don't wait for him to answer because I'm not interested in engaging him in conversation—not out here, not like this, where it's just the two of us.

In fact, where is Ron Alder, the Hemlock Inn's valet parking attendant? Usually, he's right there keeping an eye on things. Since the inn is filled with people attending the wedding, part one of the valet rush is over since they are all at the rehearsal dinner.

I made a mental note to ask Ron if he had noticed the silver Honda guy hanging around.

When I'm safely away from Mr. Honda, I turn to ask him if he's a hotel guest, but he's already inside the car.

The engine turns over, and I snap a final series of photos of him pulling out of the space and driving away.

I text Jack. *"I think I met the guy who drives the silver Honda that was following Kate."*

Chapter Five

~ *Jenna* ~

G IGI, MOM, AND I are back at Mom's house. I am relieved not to stay at Death Hall tonight.

We've changed into our pajamas and are sitting in Mom's living room drinking tea, with the corgis at our feet, when Mom casually announces that she saw the silver Honda with the cracked headlight that had been following Kate.

I cannot believe she's been holding onto that information for a good hour while we ate frozen pizzas and recapped the day's sad events.

"Tell me you did not approach that car yourself," I say.

She smiles sheepishly. "Well, I was already outside. The car was right there. Jack and I drove right past it when we arrived at the Hemlock Inn, but we were both so preoccupied with Jack having to break the news about Kate to David that I guess we had tunnel vision and missed it. And it turned out that David wasn't even at the hotel but, of course, Jack wouldn't discuss it."

"David wasn't there? Where do you think he went?"

"I don't know," Mom says. "When I asked Jack how David took the news, he said that David wasn't in the hotel room. He wasn't pleased that I talked to the silver Honda guy. That preempted everything else. Now, he's in a mood, and he's being pretty tightlipped, reminding me that this is an active investigation."

She puts air quotes around *active investigation* and rolls her eyes before elaborating on the silver Honda dude.

Gigi throws up her hands.

I say, "Mom, this guy might be Kate's killer. I know we don't know for sure, but it was totally risky to approach the car by yourself."

However, I must admit I would've done the same thing.

She frowns as she pulls her bare feet underneath her, sinking into the corner of the sofa. Aggie jumps up and makes herself comfortable on Mom's lap. Homie remains curled up on my feet.

"The guy would've driven away without *anyone* getting his license tag number if I hadn't written it down. I didn't have any other option. Sorry. Not sorry."

Gigi and I exchange a look.

"What?" Mom says. "Don't gang up on me."

Gigi's brows arch, and she brushes an imaginary piece of lint off the leg of her pajama bottoms before saying, "Well, I suppose what's done is done, but, dear, you're not invincible like that woman you write about in those books of yours."

Aggie lets loose a yodeling howl as if she's agreeing.

"Hey," Mom says as she strokes the dog's red and white head. "Whose side are you on, Missy?"

As if Aggie understands the question, she stands up, puts her short corgi front legs on Mom's shoulders, and licks her on the cheek.

"That's better," she says, ruffling the dog's fur. "Don't forget who feeds you. But speaking of that woman I write about, I didn't finish my pages because of all the excitement this evening. I'll say good night to the two of you and get some writing done before I go to bed." She nudges the little dog off her lap and stands. "Oh, wait, but first, what's the plan for tomorrow?"

I'm glad she asks because I haven't had a chance to fill her in. I glance at Gigi to see if she wants to be the bearer of the news, but she gives me a palms-up go ahead.

Thanks, Geeg.

I take a deep breath. "Despite everything, London still wants a party tomorrow night."

I can't believe she's down with canceling the wedding but still wants to have a party. Wait a minute. Yes, I can. This is London we're talking about.

"At Gracewood Hall?" Mom asks. "It's still a crime scene."

"Before Gigi and I left to come over here, Jeff Salisbury told me they might have the house cleared by tomorrow afternoon," I say. "But they might not."

Gigi huffs. "Honestly, if I'd had any idea that this socialite's wedding would be so much trouble, I would've never agreed."

"She's not a socialite, Geeg," I say. "She's a social media influencer."

"Socialite. Social media influencer." Gigi *pfffts* and waves it off. "Doesn't it boil down to the same thing? A privileged young woman behaves selfishly because she can, and people celebrate her consumerism and wastefulness."

"Not necessarily," I say. "Plenty of influencers are nice people and work for the greater good."

"I'm sure they are, but I'm not sure London falls into that category," Gigi says. "Think of all the waste. What should we do with all the food that was supposed to be served tomorrow?"

"Tess fed everyone what was supposed to be served at the rehearsal dinner," Mom says. "People ate while they waited to be interviewed by the police. We still need to do something with the food that was supposed to be served at the wedding reception so that it doesn't go to waste."

Gigi nods.

"But no party," Gigi says. "A young woman has lost her life. The party simply cannot go on. If London wants to do something, she should show some respect and donate the food to the homeless in Kate's name."

"That's a good idea," I say. "I'll talk to Tess and see if she can arrange for that to happen."

"While we're at it," Gigi says. "To be on the safe side, I

would like to have a look at the contract we negotiated with London. I believe it said we would host a rehearsal dinner, wedding, and reception. Not a generic party. Gracewood Hall's reputation is already tarnished because of the murder. I will not further sully its name by allowing an extravagant party to take place twenty-four hours later. If London wants to throw a party, she'll have to move it to a different venue."

The three of us silently regard each other. I can't read their minds. However, I'm sure we're on the same page.

"With less than a twenty-four-hour notice?" I say. "Good luck with that. Plus, there would be the added cost of renting the place and transporting the food. I don't know that any place would offer up a space gratis in exchange for publicity in the wake of all that's happened. At least not in Hemlock."

Gigi shakes her head. "I'm putting my foot down. London Brinks will have to throw her soiree elsewhere."

"Don't worry, Gigi," I say. "We're all on the same page. Canceling the wedding and then having a blowout the next day is next-level bad taste. Though, I'm not sure how London will react to our decision. I hope she doesn't throw a hissy fit and badmouth Gracewood Hall and Champagne Wedding and Event Designs. After all, I was the one who talked her into hiring Kate."

"What happened wasn't your fault," Mom says. "And no one can blame Kate…"

Mom trails off, but we can all finish her sentence in our heads. *No one can blame Kate for being murdered.*

The thought makes me shiver. Everything has gone so fast tonight that I haven't even had time to process that Kate is gone.

Kate—my smart, sassy, no-nonsense friend—is dead.

"I think I know how we can fix this without being the heavies," Mom says. "I'll ask Jack if he could not lift the crime scene until Monday. That way, deciding not to have the party is out of our hands."

"That's a good start," I say. "As long as London hasn't graduated from a person of interest to a suspect, she and Anson will leave for their honeymoon in Cabo San Lucas on Sunday. In the meantime, Ian told her not to talk about the case on her social media platforms, but I wonder how long that will last and how she'll spin it. Let me get my phone and check her socials. She had to say something to her followers since she was supposed to livestream the rehearsal dinner, and that didn't happen."

"But Ian asked her not to do that," Gigi says.

"Have you met London?" I don't mean to be sarcastic, but clearly, Gigi doesn't fully understand who we're dealing with.

Confusion clouds my grandmother's face. "Of course, I've met her."

"I'm trying to say that Ian could ask London not to say anything, but really, there's nothing he can do to stop her. It's called free speech, Geeg."

I leave the living room to grab my phone from my purse

on the kitchen table. I'm also hoping for a text from Ian, but there isn't one. I blink away the disappointment and return to the living room in time to hear Mom say, "I hope London understands that her free speech can and will be used against her. Someone needs to teach her some manners."

"And I'd like to watch that happen," I say as I slide back into my chair.

"Oh, dear." Gigi's hand flutters to the neckline of her pink pajama top. "Don't antagonize London. She might attack Blissful Beginnings as well."

"Mom's right," I interject. "We need to let Ian and Jack handle this."

"I'll text Jack now to see if he can help us," Mom says. "While I'm at it, I'll ask if he's learned the identity of the silver Honda driver."

While Mom is texting Jack, I pull up London's Instagram. The most recent reel on the grid shows London's face frozen in an ugly cry. Anson's arm is around her. In the background, I can tell they're in a room at the Hemlock Inn.

I press play.

"Y'all, something terrible has happened. My beloved maid of honor, my oldest friend, my life-long bestie, was brutally murdered tonight, right before my rehearsal dinner started."

She pulls away from Anson. "Y'all, I can't believe it. Who would do something like this? I am out of my mind with grief. I literally can't stop crying." She spends a good thirty seconds crying for the camera. "I mean, my wedding is ruined." After a few more breathy sobs, she asks, "Or is it? This just came to me. Like Kate is whispering in my ear. Not literally, but you know what I mean. Give me a minute to let this sink in. But tell me, do you think Anson and I should go on with the nups, like tomorrow? I mean, we're here anyway. I think it might be what Kate would want us to do. But you decide. Yes or no? Hit me up with your vote in the comments."

I read aloud the first few hashtags. "#Lo-An_wedding, #Lo-An-nups, #partykiller, #shouldtheweddinggoon???, #lovewillwin, #hatemeanpeople, #nokillersallowed."

We all look at each other and cringe.

"I can't believe she would even consider holding the wedding right now," Mom says. "And she's asking her followers to vote on it?"

I'm reading the comments, which are a mix of people urging that life goes on and that she should have her wedding to spite the killer and others admonishing her for not respecting the dead. A few people even ask if she killed Kate.

In the middle of this, an alert pops up that London Brinks is live on Instagram.

I click over to the livestream and see London standing in front of a black backdrop with WHO KILLED KATE? spelled out in neon-yellow lettering. #WHOKILLEDKATE is written in black on thin yellow ribbons mimicking crime scene tape.

"Guys." She breathes the word like a sigh. "I've been

thinking. Even though you can't wait to see me and Anson get married, the wedding will have to wait." She turns and says, presumably to Anson, who is off camera, "No offense, babe. You know I have mad love for you, and I want to marry you, but first things first."

Mom and Gigi crowd around me in time to see London turn back to the camera and ask, "Who killed Kate?" She's quiet for a moment, staring at the camera with a solemn but determined expression. "Y'all, I've decided we have to help the police get to the bottom of this. We have to do this for Kate, and I need all y'all's help." She pauses again, and a single tear rolls down her cheek.

"London, stop," I say. "What are you doing?"

"That's why I'm offering ten thousand dollars to the first person who gives up any information leading to the conviction of the freak who murdered my Kate." She squints at the camera and then looks annoyed.

I realize she's reading comments.

"No, I will not give you more information about the crime. If you know, you know. And if you know, you owe it to Kate and me to find out the horrible person who did this to Kate and ruined what was supposed to be the happiest day of my life.

"Do you hear me, murderer, whoever you are? You are on notice. Kate will haunt you in your sleep and London Brinks is coming for you in real life. There will be no place that you can hide."

A second later, London holds up both hands and shakes her head. Looking straight into the camera, she dissolves into another ugly cry. After four shuddering sobs, she says, "I just can't even."

The stream ends.

"What the heck did I just see?" Mom asks.

"Oh, dear," Gigi says. "I'm not sure if that was for Kate or if London was doing it for the attention."

"Or maybe it was a big gesture to take the heat off her," Mom says. "She's the one who found the body, which makes her one of the main persons of interest in the case."

Mom is typing something on her phone. She frowns and makes a *tsking* sound. "Even if this little stunt is meant to divert attention off herself, she's still getting a lot of attention. I mean, look at this." She holds up her phone and shows us the search results for *London Brinks's wedding*. Headlines such as *Social Media Influencer Offers Reward for Killer of Best Friend* and *Influencer Shares Grief Over Friend's Murder* and *Dream Wedding in Tatters After Murder Shakes the TikToksphere*.

"Do you think she would sabotage her own wedding to gain sympathy and followers?" Mom asks. "I know it's pretty farfetched."

"It would be a horrendous publicity stunt that only a sociopath could pull off," I say.

"However, knowing what we know about London," Gigi says, "it's not out of the realm of possibility. Think about it.

The bride's big day is thwarted because her maid of honor is killed right before an elaborate wedding that was meant to be livestreamed to her three million followers. It would also create a convenient excuse not to marry Anson. The two don't seem to like each other very much."

The more I think about it, the more I realize London would have everything to gain if she could pull off a stunt of this magnitude. She'd already gotten an all-expense paid vacation, a cocktail party, and a free Cabo San Lucas honeymoon. She looks like the injured party since her fairy-tale wedding was ruined.

She mentioned a force majeure clause in the contracts, which would take effect if the wedding was shut down by forces beyond her control—such as the police declaring the venue a crime scene. Unlike most brides who would be on the hook for the cost of a luxurious wedding, London can walk away, and it won't cost her a dime.

"Stranger things have happened," Mom says.

"I don't think she would murder someone for that," I say. "But have you considered that the sabotage might've been aimed at us?"

I hold up my phone and show them another article: *The Curse of Fabled Gracewood Hall Strikes Again.*

Gigi gasps. "Oh, no. What does it say?"

I pull up the article and pass my phone to Gigi so she can read it.

"You purchased Gracewood Hall before it went on the

market. Do you know anyone who might've been disgruntled over not getting a chance to bid on it?"

Gigi looks up from the phone. Her eyes are wide. "Heavens, I don't know. The purchase seemed pretty straightforward to me. Linda Conti Stanton's estate was ready to sell the place, and I had the cash to purchase it. It seemed like an easy enough transaction. Do you think someone would be mad enough to murder an innocent woman over it?"

Mom shrugs. "I hope not." She reaches into the end table's drawer, takes out a legal pad and pen, and writes down something.

"Someone sabotaging us is a longshot, but it's an angle," she says. "We also shouldn't discount the possibility that someone might've been out to ruin London's wedding."

"But why kill Kate?" I ask. "Why not London?" I grimace.

It's not that I want London to die. I'd never wish that on anyone. But as my mother said, it's an angle that we need to consider.

"We don't know London that well," Mom says, "but even in the short time we've worked with her to make her wedding happen, we've seen her upset plenty of people."

"It could've been someone who wanted to attend the wedding but wasn't invited," Gigi suggests.

Mom points at her with her pen. "Yes. That's a possibility." She adds it to the list.

Gigi's eyes sparkle. "Is this how you plot those mystery books you write?"

"I wish this was a story plot," Mom answers.

"I know. I don't mean to be insensitive. I was feeling sort of helpless given all that's happened, but thinking about possible suspects certainly puts some of the power back in our hands. Doesn't it?"

Mom and I nod. We know about that all too well. We've helped solve three previous cases that happened right here in Hemlock. Jack wasn't very happy about us getting involved, but he still wants to marry Mom despite it all. Unless he's completely delusional, he has to know that she won't give up sleuthing just because she's marrying the chief of police.

We won't let each other wander into danger alone. So, Jack has both of us to contend with in that regard. Now, he might even have Gigi. Strength in numbers.

"Who else is on our list?" Gigi asks.

Before Mom can read off the suspects, her phone rings.

"It's Jack," she says. "I need to take this."

"Of course you do," Gigi says with a twinkle in her eyes. "Since it looks like we're in for a late night, I'll make some popcorn for us."

Gigi pads off to the kitchen. I follow her to help and to give my mom some privacy.

My grandmother is in love with being in love. It is no surprise that she was ecstatic to meet Jack and learn that he and Mom are engaged. Gigi said she'd always love my father like a son and mourn his loss, but Mom is too young to spend the rest of her life alone.

Before the kernels begin to pop, Mom appears in the kitchen looking annoyed.

"That was quick," I say.

She nods. "Jack is happy to keep the crime scene in place for an extra day. Of course, that means we can't go on the property, but that will give us another night together."

She smiles, and I realize how much I miss living near her. I guess in a lot of ways I took it for granted. I didn't mean to. It was because … life. I mean, when I lived downstairs, we would sometimes have a cup of late-night tea together and discuss the plots of her books … or in the rare instances when we'd been drawn into a local crime, we'd do exactly what we're doing tonight.

It's bittersweet. I wish we could have more of these nights.

I do love living with Gigi at Gracewood Hall—or at least I did. Honestly, now it feels a little spooky. But I'll get over it. I have to because after Mom and Jack get married, they don't need Mom's twenty-seven-year-old daughter hanging around.

I'm happy for her … for them. I really am.

But all those years we were waiting to learn my father's fate, it was just the two of us.

Of course, I have Ian. Sort of. Things are good between us, even if they're still up in the air. But that's a story for a different day. Right now, over the sound of the air popper, my mom says that Jack ran a check on the silver Honda's tags, but he won't tell her what he found out.

What?

That's weird. He's always shared info with Mom, even if she had to get it out of him by playing the hypothetical game. She'd ask him questions about the case, starting with the words, *hypothetically speaking.*

Hypothetically speaking, if there's a car in my story—let's say it was a silver Honda—and it's following someone. What would the driver's name be? Hypothetically.

"I'm so upset right now," Mom says. "He wouldn't have that license tag number if not for me."

Gigi and I are quiet.

Mom sits at the table and scribbles something on the yellow legal pad she's carried into the kitchen.

"I'm sorry, honey," Gigi says. "Maybe he couldn't share it because he was around his coworkers. Is he coming over tonight? Maybe he'll fill you in then."

"No, he's on his way to Asheville to break the news about Kate to David. That's where David lives."

Gigi tuts. "Well, at least we know why David wasn't at the Hemlock Inn. I guess he went home. Poor fellow. It's such sad news. He and Kate had found each other again. They seemed so in love."

The popcorn spills out of the popper and into the large ceramic bowl Gigi has placed in front of it. My grandmother turns away from us and gets the pan of butter she'd been melting on the stove.

Gigi turns off the popper and brings the bowl to the table.

"What are you writing?" she asks Mom.

"I'm making a list of potential suspects. Let's go back over the timeline, beginning with when Kate arrived. Jenna, do you want to go first?"

I think as I chew the popcorn I put into my mouth right before Mom asked me the question. Things were so hectic…

"From the time Kate arrived, she was freaked out because that silver car had been following her. Apparently, it wasn't the first time she'd spotted the car. I saw it. It drove onto the property and circled back out without stopping. The car's windows were tinted, and the sun hit them just right. So, I couldn't see the driver. Did you write down the silver car—even though we don't know much about it yet?"

Mom is looking down at what she's writing, but I still catch how she smirks at the mention of the car. Even though she's not talking about it much, I can sense she's stewing over Jack withholding the information.

"I did. Right here." She taps the spot on the paper with her pen.

"Kate and London went off to get their stories straight about how they know each other. We had the wedding rehearsal. Anson was being a pig flirting with Kate. Is Anson on the list?"

"He is now," Mom said.

"Good. Then, about an hour and a half before the dinner, Kate went to the hotel to change clothes. She was late getting back because she spotted the silver Honda again. She was unnerved, but I was rushing out to get London so she could hear the toast she'd asked Kate to write. I had a gut feeling that London would want to make changes, but we had less than a half hour before she and Anson were supposed to make their grand entrance at the rehearsal dinner."

"So, Anson had been flirting with Kate. A lot," Mom says.

"But that would point back to London, who is awfully volatile," Gigi says.

"Volatile, yes, but I don't think she'd murder Kate because her fiancé flirted with her," I say. "She might murder Anson."

"But what if Anson got upset with Kate for rejecting his advances?" Gigi asks, her brows arched like she's presented the winning combination in a game of Clue. *The groom did it in front of the ladies' bathroom with a champagne bottle...* That sounds vaguely dirty, so I don't say it out loud.

As I'm explaining that Anson was so drunk after doing tequila shots with that blonde that he could barely stand up, Mom's phone rings again.

I'm fully expecting the call to be from Jack, who is ready to fill Mom in on the silver Honda, but when Mom turns over her phone to check the display screen, she frowns.

"Hello?" she says and pauses. "Yes, this is Madeline Bell. What's the problem?"

Someone is talking, but I can't hear what they're saying. I'm watching my mom's gaze narrow. Her expression grows more concerned.

"It's the alarm company," she whispers to us.

When we purchased the security system, the company had to do the install in two parts. First, they alarmed the building's perimeter to keep out curiosity seekers, but they had to wait for the security cameras because Gracewood Hall needed so many they had to order them.

Since Gigi isn't tech-savvy, she asked that Mom and I be listed as the contacts in case of an alarm event … like this.

"No one is supposed to be at Gracewood Hall right now." Mom is talking to the person on the phone again.

"Absolutely no one," Gigi echoes. "Jenna and I set the alarm after the police interviewed the last party guest. That nice officer walked us to our car and followed us out the gates in his patrol car. No one should be at Gracewood Hall right now."

"Yes, please dispatch the police immediately," Mom says.

Chapter Six

~ *Maddie* ~

"ARE YOU ALL right?" Jenna asks me as we wait for the red light at the intersection of Columbus Avenue and Main Street to change. "You seem tense."

I force myself to unclench my jaw and smile, but I know it doesn't reach my eyes. "I do?"

"Yes. You do."

I have a good reason. I am still stinging from Jack's refusal to share the identity of the silver Honda driver. He didn't even call me back last night after he got home from Asheville.

"He wouldn't have the lead on the silver Honda if not for me." I hadn't meant to say that out loud. The words slipped out.

"You're still upset that he didn't share the info?" Jenna says, as if she even had to ask. "Don't be upset with Jack."

She's right. I shouldn't be offended, but his unwillingness to share offended me.

"Mom, he's in the middle of an active investigation. He's

not supposed to talk about it with anyone."

"I am not just anyone."

"You know that's not his rule. If he shares too much, it could jeopardize everything. Plus, since a killer is running around out there, I'll bet he doesn't want to take a chance on you investigating on your own and getting hurt."

"It never stopped him from talking to me before," I say. "But now that we're engaged, he suddenly clams up. It feels personal, Jenna."

"But it's not, and you have to believe that."

As I ease my black Toyota RAV4 through the intersection, Lily King, the owner of Lily's Tearoom, which is next door to my bridal salon, recognizes my car and waves hello as we pass her on Main Street. Even though I don't feel like smiling, I dig deep, force the corners of my lips upward, and wave back.

"It seems like there's more going on here than you being upset by his lack of sharing," Jenna says.

"If I marry this man, he should know me well enough to understand it's not my nature to passively sit by and wait when a crime affects me personally. I was interested in writing mysteries and solving crimes long before I met him."

"Yes, you were," Jenna says. "But … huh. How did you get interested in crime and mysteries? I can't believe I've never asked you this, but I mean, you own a bridal boutique. Crime and weddings aren't exactly synonymous."

I take a moment to ponder that question. "I don't know

if you remember this, but it started shortly after your father went missing. I was at loose ends, but trying to hold it together for you. The shop kept me busy during the day, but everything seemed so much worse at night. Gigi was in California, and you were seventeen years old. I couldn't expect you to stay home and hold my hand. I'd read every mystery at the library and could only watch so much television.

"I'd always wanted to write, but I was clueless when it came to writing a novel. One day, while I was in the library, on a whim, I posted a notice asking if others were interested in forming a mystery writers support group. I had no idea how much comfort I would get from writing. I had no control over the chaos in my real life, but I could lose myself in the world of my story. I could right wrongs and bring the perp to justice. It was the ultimate form of escapism and a lot better than medicating myself with drugs or alcohol."

"Thank goodness for that," Jenna says. "But why not confine the sleuthing to the page?"

"I'll turn that question back on you." I slant a glance and a smile at my daughter. "Why have you gotten involved in the cases you've looked into with me?"

"Touché. The ones I've looked into have always felt personal. Like this case. I don't think I will be able to butt out until Kate's killer is brought to justice. That will have to happen before Gigi and I feel comfortable moving back into Gracewood Hall. Lucky you. You're stuck with us."

"As far as I'm concerned, you can move in permanently. I love having you there."

We're silent for a moment, and then Jenna says, "I thought it was important for you to have your own space after you and Jack got engaged."

I can't sort out the weird feelings swirling inside me. Jenna must read my mind—or, more likely, my pained expression.

"Are things moving too fast for you?"

I shrug. My eyes well up, and I feel like such an idiot for crying.

"It doesn't have to be either or," Jenna says. "You don't have to get married right now, but waiting on the engagement doesn't mean you have to break up. You can just … be.

"You've spent so many years trying to make other people happy—being true to Dad, trying to protect me, trying to make Jack happy. It's okay to think of yourself for once. If you and Jack are meant to be, he'll be there for you."

I swallow hard and feel a little more in control of my emotions. "I can't expect him to wait around while I figure out my heart. That wouldn't be fair to him."

Jenna gives a one-shoulder shrug. "Well, if you want to be fair to him, you need to talk to him. Remember when I dated Owen Snow, who was so totally wrong for me, and I did everything possible to make him break up with me?"

"Owen Snow. I haven't heard that name in ages." I muse

as I turn into the police department parking lot. It's located off Catalpa Street in the town's municipal building, which also houses the jail. It's only a few blocks from my shop.

"I know, right? He was a good guy, but just not right for me and where I was in life at the time. Do you remember saying I needed to own my feelings and be honest with myself and him?"

"I do remember that." And I know exactly where she's going with this. After I park and kill the engine, I say, "I love Jack—" The rest of my words can't get past the lump in my throat.

The car's engine clicks and ticks in the silence as if saying, *but…*

I clear my throat. "It's clear that I need to do some soul-searching and figure out where these feelings are coming from. In the meantime, we need to talk about what we want to ask Betsy. Do you think she killed Kate?"

"Betsy?" Jenna's eyes widen.

"Yeah, I know. It's weird to think of her doing that to Kate. They arrested her for crossing the police line, but honestly, this is the first time I've thought that she might've been the one who killed Kate. Why would she do it? It doesn't really make sense, does it?"

"I don't know," Jenna says. "When Jeff called and said that they had Betsy in custody, it did cross my mind for a second that she might've done it. Then, I shrugged it off because it seemed so far-fetched. But why did she return to the crime scene?"

"What's her motive other than Kate replacing her as London's maid of honor?" I ask. "Betsy was irritated in the moment, but I think she was happy to have the out."

"Right," Jenna says. "She couldn't get out of there fast enough."

"Do you think Kate and Betsy knew each other before coming to Hemlock?" I ask.

"I don't know that much about Betsy," Jenna says. "I guess it's possible. Stranger things have happened. Could they have run into each other at the hotel before Kate was…" Jenna's voice trails off, and she swallows hard.

I touch her arm. "I'm so sorry this happened to Kate. If you don't feel like going in and talking to Betsy with me, I can take you home and come back."

My daughter takes a deep breath. "No. We're already here. I think it's important that both of us talk to her. One of us might pick up on something the other misses."

"Are you sure?" I ask. "I don't mind taking you home."

"No, I'm fine. If nothing else, I'll do this for Kate. So, come on. Let's go in there and ask Betsy why she broke into Gracewood Hall last night."

~ *Jenna* ~

INSIDE THE POLICE station, it takes Ina Gerardi, the Hemlock Police Department front desk manager, a while to ascertain if Betsy Rutt wants to see us.

"Is the chief in?" Mom asks.

"Nope, hon, sorry," Ina says. "He's out at Gracewood Hall where that murder happened last night. Such a shame, isn't it? Guess I don't have to tell you that since it's Gigi's place."

Mom and I nod.

"I can remember a time not so long ago when people in these parts used to sleep with their doors unlocked and their windows wide open." Marge Harney walks up behind us to join us at Ina's desk. It was as if she materialized from out of nowhere.

"What's the latest, ladies?" Marge has a habit of clicking her tongue at the start of every sentence. "Have they caught the killer yet? It's so unnerving. I didn't get a wink of sleep last night."

"I don't know, Marge," Mom says. "Gracewood Hall is still considered a crime scene."

"Sakes alive." Her hand flutters to the neckline of her ocher cotton jersey dress. "Maddie, I thought you, of all people, would have the inside scoop since you're engaged to the chief."

Mom's mouth flattens into a line. I know she's thinking about how Jack won't tell her what's happening.

As a commanding officer of Hemlock's illustrious gossip brigade—the vehicle that gathers and disseminates all the latest Hemlock happenings to any who will listen—Mrs. Harney gets most of her munition from stealth maneuvers like this.

And from asking shameless questions.

The running joke around town is what the gossip brigade can't ferret out, they make up, which is always a concern.

"Your poor, poor mama," Marge says. "Such a shame that this had to happen at her new home. How is Gigi holding up?"

"She's doing well, considering," Mom says. "She's staying with me for the time being."

"You're a good girl, Maddie," Marge says. "What a terrible welcome home for her. If it were me, I'd have to take to the bed until all this was settled. It's too much. That's what brings me in today. Ina, I want to start a neighborhood watch group. We can't be too careful these days. Can I count on your support, ladies?"

"Of course," we all say.

"The Ladies League meets soon," I add. "Why don't you ask to have the topic put on the agenda."

"Jenna Bell, you're not only lovely but also one smart cookie." Marge sighs. "That's probably why you're still single. Guys get intimidated when a young lady has looks and brains."

I have to bite the insides of my cheeks to keep a straight face or from blurting about how, in that one sentence, she'd set our gender back decades.

"Are you still going with Val's nephew … what was his name?"

"His name is Ian McCoy," I say.

"Yes. Isn't he a lawyer out of Asheville or some such? I think I heard that somewhere."

"He is," I say, sticking to the bare minimum.

"That's good. If he's a professional, he's probably secure enough in himself." Her eyes sparkle. "Maybe we'll hear wedding bells sooner rather than later. Aren't you in your thirties by now?"

I freeze. I'm sure a stupid grin is plastered on my face.

"Marge, why don't you stop by the house sometime soon," Mom says. "I know Gigi would love to see you."

Thanks, Mom! You are a goddess among mothers for getting her off my case.

"I will do that," she says, dropping the subject of my spinsterhood like it's old news. "Ina, be a dear and give me a stack of these brochures so I can hand them out at the next Ladies League meeting."

Ina complies, and Mrs. Harney tucks the pamphlets inside her purse. "I'd better run. I need to get Lawton's dinner cooking. You tell Gigi I'll call on her soon."

"I'll do that, Marge," Mom says. "I'm sure she'd love to see you and catch up."

We watch the glass door close behind her, and we look at each other and laugh.

Mom seems more relaxed now. I'm sure it's thanks in

part to Mrs. Harney's antics, but it's probably because she knows Jack isn't here right now. I'm breathing a little easier, too. After the way they left things last night, I'm sure he won't be very happy that we were here talking to Betsy. Even though she broke into Gracewood Hall, which is totally our business.

We're here to talk to her and decide whether to press charges.

Yep, that's our story, and we're sticking to it.

And if we ask Betsy a couple of questions that lean more toward Kate's murder … what can he do? Arrest us?

While we're waiting to go back and talk to Betsy, I text London. *"How are you holding up?"*

She answers, *"#freeLondonBrinks"*

"Did the police arrest you?"

"OMG NO! h8 my life stuck in hemlock prisoner of the system   #freeLondonBrinks   #missedflighttocabo #AHHHHHHHH"

I start to tell her that it could be a lot worse than being stuck at the Hemlock Inn. The police can't force her to stay unless they arrest her, but I decide against saying too much. That's Ian's department. The last thing he needs is me planting ideas in London Brinks's hard head.

"I saw your livestream yesterday."

She answers, *"GR8 huh?!!!!"*

I blink at the words. I'm not sure *G R 8* is how I would describe it—like it was an award-worthy documentary.

I type, *"I'm sure your heart is in the right place, but be careful. You told a murderer you're coming for them. You might be in their crosshairs."*

"cnt stp thnkng bout K8 have platform wanna do g00d lets bring dwn K8s killer together gotta bounce TTYL #whokilledkate <kiss emojis>"

I hold out the phone to Mom. "Look at this."

She reads the text conversation and shakes her head. "She does not live in the real world." Mom hands me back my phone. "Did London kill Kate?" she asks. "Maybe she lashed out at Kate after she refused to change the toast? She had a champagne bottle when she went downstairs. Maybe she didn't intend to kill her. She might've had an angry outburst."

"Yeah, but the champagne bottle was only half-full, and London was pretty lit. I don't know if she'd have the strength or the aim in that condition. I guess we'll have to wait for the lab results to come back. Time will tell."

About twenty minutes later, an officer appears to take us back to talk to Betsy. He checks our purses and phones. He instructs us to walk through a weapons detection system and finally buzzes us through the security door separating the lobby from the offices and holding area.

We follow him down a linoleum hallway lit by buzzing fluorescent bulbs that bathe everything in a ghoulish green glow. We are ushered into a room where Betsy is waiting behind a thick wall of bulletproof glass.

Even though I was born and raised in Hemlock, I've only seen this side of the police station once. That was when I was the chief suspect after my ex-boyfriend was murdered. Thanks to some quick thinking on Mom's part and solid reasons why-not, I wasn't a suspect very long.

I hope with all my heart that's the case for Betsy... If she didn't murder Kate.

"Did you bring my bracelet?" Betsy looks worn out.

She has dark circles under her eyes. Her brassy hair looks limp and greasy. Her pale skin appears grayer than when she wore the chartreuse maid-of-honor dress.

"What bracelet?" Mom asks.

"The bracelet that got me arrested," she snaps and then seems to check herself. "It's my charm bracelet. London wouldn't let me wear it with my bridesmaid dress. I took it off and left it on the shelf in the changing room. After London kicked me out of the wedding, I was so angry, and in such a hurry to leave, I forgot that I'd left it in the bride's room. I don't think you were in the room when it happened, but right before London threw a fit over the nail polish, she made me take off my bracelet and wear the one some jewelry designer made for her wedding. She said there would be no jewelry in the wedding unless a sponsor provided it." Betsy rolls her eyes.

She seems awfully calm for a person who spent the night in jail.

"You trespassed through a designated crime scene and set

off the alarm system at Gracewood Hall for a charm bracelet?" I ask.

"Yes. My grandmother gave me that bracelet. Every charm means something special," she says. "I wanted it back. I had no idea that someone had been murdered."

"Even though the place was covered in crime scene tape," Mom deadpans.

"I thought the crime scene tape was one of London's publicity stunts. She's so tacky she'd totally do something like that. Look, I've told the police all of this. They said they'd check out my story and see if the bracelet is where I left it. Spoiler alert—it will be there. Yet, they're taking their sweet time verifying that my story checks out."

"Well, they did arrest you for trespassing on a crime scene," Mom says. "They're probably checking your alibi. You do have one, don't you?"

"For the record, I didn't do it," Betsy says. "I've never met the dead girl."

I wince.

The fact that Betsy skirted the question about her alibi doesn't escape me.

"Okay, but why did you break into Gracewood Hall? If you wanted your bracelet, you could've popped in last night while the rehearsal dinner was going on or come by today to pick it up."

"I didn't want to risk seeing London," she says. "After she kicked me out of the wedding, she also banned me from all the festivities. Nice, huh? Anson is my brother. She pulls this, and they're not even married. Can you imagine what she'll be like after they make this legally binding?" Betsy rolls her eyes again. "*If* they make this legally binding," Betsy says. "Big emphasis on the *if*. They're not married yet."

I slant a glance at Mom. I know she's wondering the same thing I'm wondering. Would Betsy stoop to murder to stop her brother from marrying London?

Betsy has a motive. Her sister-in-law-to-be is a monster who kicked her out of the wedding and seems to have her brother cowed. Plus, she'd broken into Gracewood Hall.

I make a mental note to add it to the list.

"I was supposed to go home today," Betsy says. "I booked a flight that was leaving at nine o'clock this morning. Then I realized that I'd left my bracelet in the dressing room. I had to get it last night. I had no choice."

I have so many questions, but Betsy is on a roll, so it's best to let her keep talking.

"I knocked on the door at Gracewood Hall, but no one answered. So, I walked around to the back of the place to see if anyone in the building could let me in. I tried all the doors, and one was open. So, I went in."

She shrugs.

That seems awfully convenient. I glance at Mom, but she's wearing her poker face, and her gaze is pinned on Betsy. All I know is the police secured the premises before Gigi and I left. It's unlikely they'd leave a door open.

"Why didn't you ask a family member to get it for you?" I ask.

"*Ugh*, my parents. They're so mad at me. Even if I could get out of here today, which I can't, I would have to go before a judge on Monday. But before all this happened, I didn't want to ask my parents to get the bracelet because that would've been another reminder that London had kicked me out of the wedding. Things are tense enough. I didn't want to ruin my brother's wedding by drawing more attention to the fact that their future daughter-in-law is a *bee-otch*."

"You didn't want to ruin the wedding?" Mom asks. "Why not? You've made it clear that you don't like London. Wouldn't this have been the perfect opportunity to seek revenge?"

"You think I would take revenge by killing someone?" Betsy recoils, her eyes huge. "I'm vegan. I don't kill. Period."

That might be her best defense. I want to believe her, but—"You didn't answer me a moment ago when I asked you if you have an alibi for earlier in the night when Kate was killed."

"I was in my room at the Hemlock Inn. I ordered up room service." Betsy shrugs. "The hotel has security footage. They should be able to confirm that I left when I said I did. If Gracewood Hall had cameras, you'd already know I was telling the truth."

She's right, but we can't go back in time.

"How do you know we don't have security cameras?"

Mom asks.

Good question. That's why she writes the mysteries, and I tag along.

"The police told me when I asked them to check Gracewood Hall footage. Look, I'll tell you exactly what I told the police. I took an Uber to Gracewood Hall around eleven thirty last night. I figured the dinner would be over, and everyone would be gone since the wedding was the next day. The driver's name was Rupert. He was there when the police arrived. They've already interviewed him.

"Speaking of the police." She grimaced and seemed to shrink into herself. "They said the breaking and entering charges were up to you as the property owner. I just wanted my bracelet. Thinking about it now, I know it was a dumb thing to do, but I thought I could get in there and get out without upsetting anyone. I didn't mean any harm. You have to believe me."

When neither Mom nor I say anything, Betsy leans in and puts her hand on the glass.

"Crossing a police line is a misdemeanor, but breaking and entering is a felony," she says. "I'm not too proud to beg. Please don't press charges."

An officer enters the room. "I'm sorry, ladies. Your time is up. I need to escort Ms. Rutt back to her cell."

Betsy says something, but we can't hear what she says. It appears that they must've turned off the two-way microphone. As the officer cuffs her, Betsy throws us a terrified, pleading glance.

As the officer who ushered us in helps us retrace our path down the green-lit linoleum hallway, I say, "It was kind of mean to leave without the promise that you'll not press charges."

When Mom doesn't answer me, I ask, "You're not pressing charges, are you?"

"It's not up to me. It's Gigi's decision since she's the property owner. However, I'm inclined to think that as long as the police don't charge her with Kate's murder, then Gigi won't press charges."

I hadn't thought of it but… "That is true."

We walk in silence the rest of the way. As we approach the exit, my phone sounds a text notification. Hoping it's Ian, I check.

"Oh, my gosh." I stop in my tracks.

It's not him, but it's a close second.

"What's wrong?" Mom asks.

"Nothing is wrong," I say. "In fact, everything just got a whole lot better."

"What do you mean?"

I glance around to see who's within earshot.

I don't want to chance it, so I say, "Let's get in the car and I'll tell you."

When we're safely tucked inside Mom's RAV4, she asks, "What's going on?"

"Hold on, a second. I need to make a call."

I place a call to my friend Greta Finster. In college, she was simply known as Finster, the computer genius.

"Hey, Fins," I say. "I got your text. Do you have something for me?"

"Indeed, I do."

"Hold on, let me get a pen and paper to write on."

I jot down the information Finster has for me.

"Thanks, friend. I owe you big time."

After I hang up, Mom asks, "What's going on?"

"Finster found out the name and the address of the guy who drives the silver Honda."

Chapter Seven

~ Maddie ~

WE NOW KNOW that the silver Honda owner's name is Greg Paulson. He lives in Greenville, South Carolina.

We don't know if this is the guy who was following Kate and, if so, why he was tailing her.

We can't do anything with the silver Honda information—yet—but we are close to the hotel. So, we might as well make the most of our time.

Still buzzing over the silver car intel that Jenna obtained, we leave the police station and go to the Hemlock Inn, which is located at the opposite end of Main Street from my shop, to talk to Sabrina Parsons, the hotel's manager.

When we get there, she is helping a guest. So, we hang back.

"I still can't believe you got the goods on the guy who drives the silver Honda," I say.

Jenna smiles. "Since Jack hasn't been very forthcoming, I figured we needed a workaround to help us get the driver's info. I didn't tell you I was working on it because I wasn't one hundred percent sure Finster would be able to deliver, but I figured it was worth a try."

Just when I think my daughter can't impress me more, she does. "Clearly, it worked. Dare I ask how you did it?"

"Do you really want to know?" she asks.

"Probably not but tell me anyway."

She glances around, but the lobby is mostly empty. "I may or may not know someone who knows someone with skills." She puts air quotes around the last word.

"Such as how to get into the state's department of motor vehicles computer system through the back door?" I ask.

"Wow, that sounds super illegal. So, I probably shouldn't say one way or the other."

"You're probably right," I say. "The fewer details I know, the better. The bottom line is even though Jack may not be able to talk to us about the investigation, it doesn't mean that we can't proceed with our own inquiry."

"Exactly," Jenna says. "You seemed so down last night after you talked to him that I had to do something to help brighten your mood."

A sigh escapes before I can stop it. "Thank you, sweet girl. You know me so well. I refuse to sit around and mope or wait. That's not who I am."

We're quiet for a moment. Then Jenna asks, "Do you think you should text Jack to tell him we were at the police station? You know he'll find out. It might be better if he hears it from you."

She's right. I should let him know. On the one hand, if I tell him, he probably won't be very happy with me. On the other hand, if I don't tell him … he won't be very happy with me. I stand up to ward off the anxiety.

"Are you okay?" Jenna asks. "I didn't mean to upset you."

"It's okay. You're right. I need to tell him. It's all in how I say it."

I sit down and text him.

"Hey, Jenna and I stopped by the station to talk to Betsy Rutt. We're trying to figure out if we will press charges. Sorry we missed you."

I hold out the phone and show the message to my daughter.

"Perfect," she says.

I hope it will be an icebreaker. I haven't heard from Jack since he put me in my place last night. I know he's busy, but I stare at my phone hoping to see the dancing bubbles indicating he's typing a reply. The screen is lifeless.

"Hey, ladies." Sabrina waves us over.

Not a moment too soon. I shove my phone in my purse and stand.

"Hi, Sabrina," I say. "How's everything at the Hemlock Inn?"

"It's finally settling down," she says. "Most of the wedding guests checked out early this morning. This is the first time I've had a moment to catch my breath."

"I imagine they want to get out of town while the getting is good," I say.

"Before the chief can pull them back in," Jenna clarifies. "I hope they know that if he needs to see them again, they'll have to come back. But I would imagine that most of them have been cleared."

"Uh-huh," Sabrina says. "I don't suppose the murder at Gracewood Hall is what brings you two in here today?"

"We might be looking into the case," I say.

Sabrina smiles. "I'd be disappointed if you weren't."

Jenna and I grin at each other.

"Do you have a moment?" Jenna asks. "We're hoping you can help us."

"I always have time for you two," Sabrina says.

Sabrina is an avid mystery reader who has expressed an interest in writing a book someday. I had a feeling she would see this as an opportunity to possibly help solve a crime rather than defying Jack's mandate to not interfere with an investigation.

I'm glad we're on the same page.

"Let me get someone to cover the front desk for me, and we can go into the office," she says. "Would you like some coffee?"

A few moments later, we've settled into Sabrina's office. The space isn't large, but in addition to the desk, which holds her computer and stacks of paper that look like reports, there's enough room for a cozy grouping of a loveseat and two winged-back chairs. As Jenna and I choose the two chairs, someone knocks on the door. It's a guy from the food service staff with a tray bearing a silver pot of coffee, which he sets on the coffee table and pours into three white china cups before leaving us alone.

Sabrina slides onto the loveseat and gestures to the sugar bowl and cream pitcher. "I wasn't sure how you take your coffee. Please help yourself."

Soon, Jenna holds up her phone and shows Sabrina a photo of David, which she pulled from a Google search.

"Do you remember seeing this guy around the hotel yesterday?"

"May I?" Sabrina asks.

Jenna hands her the phone.

"Oh, this guy again." Sabrina shakes her head. "The chief showed me his photo last night and asked me how many key cards had been issued for the room. Only one key. I didn't see him, but there were a lot of people in and out this week because of the wedding. That doesn't mean he wasn't here. Who is he? Jack didn't tell me, and I didn't want to ask."

"He is—or, I guess I should say, was—" I'm surprised by the well of emotion that steals my words, especially when I didn't know Kate.

But I can't stop thinking that she was Jenna's age. Jenna's friend. Kate had her whole life ahead of her, but I won't bring her killer to justice by getting weepy on behalf of all the moms of promising young women who didn't get the chance they deserved.

I take a deep breath and clear my throat. "He was the boyfriend of the victim, Kate Asher. I think he was supposed to be waiting for Kate in her room while she was at the wedding."

"Hmm… May I share something in confidence?" Sabrina asks.

"Yes," Jenna and I say at the same time.

"The chief said David wasn't in the room when they went up there last night. Kate's room was empty. They asked me to call them if he returned."

"Didn't they have an officer posted outside the door?" Jenna asks.

"They still do," Sabrina says.

Darn. That means we can't go up and have a nose around.

"Apparently, the woman's sister is coming to town to identify the body and get her belongings. The chief indicated they'd have someone at the room's door until then. But—" Questions dance in Sabrina's eyes.

"What?" I ask.

"I overheard one officer talking to another." She raises her brows, and her eyes get large, as if what she has to say is so big that it will pop out of her. "Apparently, they found a rather large amount of cash in her room. Like twenty grand."

"Really?" Jenna says.

Why would Kate be carrying around that much cash? Even if London paid her for being her maid of honor, it would've been a fraction of that amount.

"So, now the owners of the Hemlock Inn are worried that she was a high-class call girl or something like that," Sabrina says. "They don't want that kind of shady business going on around here."

"No worries, that's not what was going on," I say. "Kate was a bridesmaid for hire. London Brinks hired her to be her maid of honor."

Sabrina's mouth falls open.

"Please, don't tell anyone," Jenna says. "London's story was that Kate was her lifelong best friend, and Kate didn't think she'd be able to attend the wedding, but at the last moment, her schedule opened up. We will have a big mess on our hands if word gets out that the queen of social media had to hire a friend."

Sabrina made a face. "Yep. I've dealt with Ms. Brinks on several occasions this week. Let's just say … I understand."

The three of us exchange knowing glances.

"Did you see anyone or anything strange this week?"

"Nothing stranger than usual. This is a hotel. We run a class establishment, but I still see some things." Sabrina tucks a strand of auburn hair behind her ear.

I show her the photo of Greg Paulson and ask if she noticed him hanging around the hotel, but I strike out again. "I haven't seen him before. You might want to ask the parking attendants and porters. That's their domain, but I can't guarantee you how discreet they'll be. The police have already interviewed them, and I had to ask them to stop talking about it in front of our guests. Even though the murder didn't happen here, it's bad enough that the killer might've been staying at the hotel."

I know that Sabrina is thinking about the time that a murder did happen at the hotel. That sad incident hasn't been far from my mind because the victim in that case was a friend of mine.

"With the police up there guarding the room, I don't suppose there's a way to sneak in," Jenna asks. "Just to take a peek?"

Sabrina holds up her hands. "You know I'd help if I could, but that sounds dangerously close to breaking the law."

"And we would never ask you to do that," I say. "However, I do have another big ask."

Sabrina grimaces. "One that won't get me arrested, I hope."

"It will not get you arrested, but it might be a little…" I shrug and scrunch my face so I don't have to finish the sentence.

Sabrina tilts her head to the side. "What is it?"

"Is there any way we could get a look at the hotel's security camera footage?" I ask.

Sabrina draws in an audible breath and then bites her bottom lip. "I don't know, Maddie. The police have been looking at it, and Jack has made it clear that this is an—"

"Active investigation," I finish. "I know. The chief has made that abundantly clear to me, too."

Sabrina squints at me. "And you're still looking into the case?"

"You bet I am. The victim was a friend, and the murder happened at Gracewood Hall."

Sabrina smiles. "Good for you."

Heavy silence hangs in the air. Then Sabrina stands, walks to her desk, and pulls out a notebook.

"Maddie, the security footage is stored on the cloud. It's accessed through a password-protected website." She opens the notebook and thumbs through its pages.

"I'm sorry, I simply can't give you the password. I could get fired for doing that."

She holds up the notebook and points to a passage.

From where I'm sitting, I can read that the entry is United Security Systems. I can also see what appears to be a web address and more writing.

She places the open notebook on the desk and then looks at her watch.

"Oh, would you look at the time," she says. "I need to get back to work. They make such good coffee here, don't they? Feel free to have a second cup and…" She inclines her head toward the notebook and smiles, then walks to the office door, pausing and looking back at us. "Isn't it amazing all the investigating you can do on home computers these days if you know where to look? You've got to love technology."

~ Maddie ~

MONDAY MORNING, I go to the Briar Patch to write.

I almost talked myself out of it, but I needed a distraction.

Plus, it wouldn't hurt to write a few pages. Since everything that's happened, I've been distracted. I've fallen even further behind on my daily page count, and the due date is ticking ever closer at an alarming rate.

I wrote the first five books without a deadline. Now that I'm under contract, I don't want to deliver book six late. It would be so unprofessional.

On Saturday, as soon as Sabrin left us alone in the office, Jenna and I were on our feet taking photos of the notebook page with the cameras on our phones.

We haven't logged into the site that would allow us to access the security footage because Jenna had raised the question about whether the website can log our IP address, alerting John and Shirley English, the owners of the Hemlock Inn, that someone outside of the hotel had logged in.

While it wasn't illegal for us to log in with the password, if the Englishes learned Jenna and I were the culprits, they would only have to draw a short line to connect us to Sabrina.

The last thing we want to do is get her fired.

Out of an abundance of caution, Jenna placed an SOS to her tech friend Finster to ask if our IP address could be traced and, if so, if there was a way to remain anonymous.

Now, it's Monday morning, and we're still waiting to hear from Finster.

Plus, things have gone from bad to worse with Jack.

After I got home from talking to Sabrina at the hotel, Jack sent a curt text saying he wished I would've told him before I went to the police station to talk to Betsy. He said it wasn't a good look for his fiancée to be there questioning a person of interest.

The cherry on top was that he was annoyed that curiosity seekers have started gathering on the street that fronts Gracewood Hall. As if I'd invited everyone.

After a quick internet search, I discovered that, sure enough, vloggers, bloggers, and reporters had already gotten wind of the tragedy and were saying if you add the tragic Stanton love story and a murder at the first event held at Gracewood Hall, the place must be cursed.

Lovely.

Clearly, I did not leak the story. I texted him back and asked him if he wanted me to come to Gracewood Hall and handle it. He told me in no uncertain terms to stay away.

Even though my heart was breaking over Jack and this icy wall that seemed to be growing between us. I didn't answer him.

And he didn't call or text me back. It's been a long time since we've gone more than twenty-four hours without speaking—or seeing each other.

I started to reply to his text a dozen times, but I knew each incarnation of my response—each I don't have to explain myself or seek your permission—or stay at home in my place like a dutiful little wife-to-be—would only escalate what had already become a heart-wrenching disagreement.

I decided that the best response was no response.

This morning, as I debated whether or not to go to the Briar Patch Bakery, I had to keep reminding myself that Jack and I have always worked best when discussing things face-to-face. Once he catches Kate's killer, he'll be less stressed, and things will improve.

In the meantime, I sit at my usual table at the Briar Patch, knowing it's unlikely he'll stop by while he's up to his eyebrows in the investigation.

I sure would feel better if he'd pop in and let me know that everything is okay.

That we're okay.

Yes, despite my dithering heart that can't decide if I want to get married again, when the chips are down like this, I know I don't want to lose him.

The bells on the bakery door chime, and my heart leaps into my throat. Then it plummets when Mary Sue Calahan—not Jack—walks through the door.

We lock gazes.

Don't come over here.

Don't come over here.

No offense to Mary Sue. I'm just not in the mood to talk to people this morning because they're bound to ask me questions about the murder at Gracewood Hall.

I force a smile that belies my disappointment, offer a quick wave, and then train my gaze on my computer, pretending to be wrapped up in what I'm writing despite not having written a substantial sentence all morning.

In my peripheral vision, I see her walk up to the counter and place an order. A few minutes later, her tall, thin figure floats toward my table.

If I didn't want to answer questions, it probably wasn't the brightest decision to write in a public place the Monday after a murder. I was so focused on meeting Jack halfway—going to the place where our relationship began. If he stopped in for coffee, he would see me sitting here, and it would be an opening for us to talk about things.

Apparently, the rest of the community sees it as an opening, too.

"Good morning, Maddie," Mary Sue says. "I just had to say how terribly sorry I am about the horrible incident at Gigi's new place. It's just shocking." She shakes her head.

"Thanks, Mary Sue." I glance at my computer screen, hoping she'll take a hint.

"Has Jack made any progress in figuring out who *done it?*"

She chuckles at her detective joke.

I smile at her. "I have no idea, Mary Sue. Jack doesn't talk about active investigations." I shrug and let my gaze linger on my computer screen.

"Oh, well, I just thought…"

"When he catches the killer, you'll probably know before I do."

That's not true. At least, I hope it's not, but I have to say something to end this conversation.

"I do hope it doesn't take too long to close the case," she says. "It was nice chatting with you, but I'll let you go so you can get back to work."

Yes, please.

"It was good to see you, Mary Sue."

As she walks away, I take a deep breath, relieved that Mary Sue disengaged so easily.

The delicious scent of dark roasted coffee puts me further at ease. Tess told me once that her secret was adding cinnamon to the coffee before she brews it. She's walking around with a carafe, offering refills to customers lingering over fresh-baked scones and the morning paper.

"Hey, Maddie," she says. "More coffee?"

"Thanks, Tess. Only half a cup. It's already 8:40, and I

need to go across the street and help Alicia get the shop ready to open at nine o'clock."

She pours the brew into my cup, sets the pot on the table, and slides into the seat across from me at my table for two. Leaning in and lowering her voice, she asks, "Anything new on the case?"

I glance around. The table next to mine is empty, and the next closest person is Roger Belvin, a college-age kid. He's wearing a pair of noise-canceling headphones as he studies.

I don't want to chance him overhearing.

"A couple of things," I whisper. "I don't want to talk about it here. Jenna and Gigi are staying with me until everything is sorted at Gracewood. Want to come over for dinner tonight and I'll fill you in?"

"I wish I could, but I have plans."

I motion for her to lean in and give her a quick update.

Her eyes widen. "We definitely need to catch up soon."

"Tess, I don't mean to disturb you." Lona Gott, who is at a table across the room, holds up a white ceramic mug and smiles like she's making a toast to the room. "Would you be a darling and refill my coffee, please?"

Lona is sitting with my neighbor, Bertha Wimberly. They've had their heads together since they walked in at eight o'clock. As members of the gossip brigade, I'm sure they've been talking about the murder. I'm surprised they haven't stopped by my table to pepper me with questions, but even they respect that I come to the Briar Patch to work.

"Be right there, Mrs. Gott." Tess turns to me. "Text me later and let me know what I can bring."

"Will do."

"Oh, and, yoo-hoo, Maddie Bell," Mrs. Wimberly calls from across the room. "Lona and I were discussing your book, *Death by Fire*."

It's book one in my Aubrey Christensen mystery series and the first of my series to be published.

"We love it and were wondering if you would be a dear and speak to our book club?"

People turn and look at me, including Roger Belvin, whose hearing seems perfectly fine despite his noise-canceling headphones. My cheeks burn. I love that she loves the book, but I don't love being the center of attention.

I get up and go to their table so we're not calling to each other across the room. "How nice of you to ask. I didn't realize you had a book club."

Tess fills both of their cups and grins at me as she walks away.

"Oh, well, we just started it," Lona says. "*Death by Fire* is our inaugural read. It will be very special to have the author at our first meeting. Are you free, say, tonight or tomorrow evening?"

"Oh, I'm sorry," I say. "I wish I could, but this week won't work. What about next week?"

"Of course," Lona says. "I'm sure you're busy with that

murder that happened at your mother's place? Isn't it just dreadful?"

"Have they caught the perp yet?" Bertha asks.

The room falls silent except for the whooshes and gurgles of the coffeemaker as it brews a fresh pot behind the front counter. I take another breath of cinnamon-laced java and feel the weight of every eye in the room on me.

I suspect this book club invitation is a ruse to corner me so they can pump me for information about the crime.

"I haven't heard any updates," I say, which is true. "The chief is being rather tight-lipped about this one."

They frown, and the rest of the Briar Patch customers return to what they had been doing.

Before I can stop myself, I ask, "What did you think of that part in the book with the fire?"

"Huh?" the ladies grunt in unison.

"The way I deal with the fire in the book?"

"Oh! Yes. Of course," Lona says. "Simply riveting."

"Absolutely," Bertha says. "I was so relieved that Aubrey didn't die in the blaze as the title suggests. You've written a real page-turner."

And there I had my answer.

The book's title might be *Death by Fire*, but there isn't an actual blaze in the book. The fire is metaphorical.

I consider calling them on it and saying we can meet after they've read the book, but I don't want to embarrass them.

Instead, I say, "I have some in-depth book club discussion questions. I can't wait to dig into them with you. Call me, and we can set up a time next week."

"Oh, well, of course," they sputter.

"I'll probably need to give the book another once-over before we meet," Lona says. "We'll be in touch with possible dates and times."

And I will not hold my breath.

I return to my table, intending to pack up.

First, I take out my phone and check my texts, hoping for one from Jenna, saying Finster had gotten back to her.

Nothing from Jenna, but my heart leaps when I see one from Jack.

"Good morning. Not sure if you're writing at the bakery this morning. I hit the ground running and won't be able to meet you. Miss you."

I miss him, too.

He's a good guy. It touches me that while he's busy solving a murder, he took the time to let me know he couldn't make it this morning, even though we didn't have plans—more like a standing date—and he'd been irritated with me yesterday.

I love the way he doesn't hold onto things like that.

Little things like this remind me that I shouldn't lose sight of how lucky I am to have him in my life.

I stare at the diamond on my left hand, grappling with this odd sense of unease plaguing me since Jack proposed.

Jack and I had just acknowledged our feelings for each other right before the navy chaplain showed up on my doorstep and confirmed Frank's death.

Even though my husband had been missing for more than nine years, I hadn't given up on him. I'd held out hope that despite the years he'd been gone, he was alive and would somehow find his way back to us with a hair-raising story of bravery and determination.

So, the confirmation of his death made the loss feel as fresh as if my husband had died that day.

Jack was so supportive. He gave me room to mourn and time to face the loss.

Even though Jack and I have been engaged for fifteen months, I'm still not sure I'm ready to commit. Especially since it feels like he expects me to trade my independence and curiosity for a more traditional life.

But Jack is such a good guy. If I'm not ready now, will I ever be?

Jenna's right, though. I need to be honest with him and myself. Since I know Jack won't pop in this morning, I pull up the photo containing the alarm monitoring company website information and the Hemlock Inn's log-in that I'd snapped in Sabrina's office yesterday and study it. I pull up the browser on my computer and type in the alarm monitoring company's website URL. I consider logging in, but I hesitate.

I wish Finster would let us know if anyone would be able

to pinpoint that I was the one signing in.

But maybe I didn't need to wait for Finster…

I google the question. *Do websites where you view security footage record the IP addresses of those logging in?*

Much to my dismay, the consensus appears to be yes. IP addresses are public, and every website records them.

I recoil like the search engine can read my mind and knows why I asked, which I know is ridiculous.

I take a deep breath and type *Is there a way to mask an IP address?*

Chapter Eight

~ Jenna ~

"You know Chief Bradley, don't you, Jenna?" London asks.

She's wearing a neon orange and hot pink tankini bathing suit and rubbing tanning oil on her body poolside at the Hemlock Inn. "You tell him, if he doesn't release me soon, I'll make him pay my hotel bill."

I'd like to see you try.

I don't say that, of course. Instead, I conjure my most beatific smile even though I am not wearing a bathing suit. I'm dressed in black pants and a black-and-white print top that felt appropriate this morning, but now it feels like it's pulling every drop of humidity in the air under my clothes, turning them into tiny beads of sweat that are rolling down my back in rivulets.

We're off to an unseasonably warm spring.

"At least you can enjoy this gorgeous pool," I say, pacifying her like I would a whiny child, but my patience is running thin.

I've been at London's beck and call all day yesterday and for the better part of this morning. Technically, I don't have to be here, but Jack still hasn't arrested her or told her she can go. He hasn't received the results back from the lab that is analyzing the broken champagne bottle and the dress she'd been wearing when she discovered Kate's body.

While she's in limbo, I'd rather keep an eye on her than chance her skipping town, but that doesn't mean I have to babysit her twenty-four-seven.

"Technically, the police cannot make me stay here," she says as she hands the brown bottle of tanning oil to Anson and turns over onto her stomach. Obediently, he pours the product into his hands and applies it to her back, but while he rubs, his gaze strays to a tanned brunette in a tiny white bikini who is emerging from the pool via the shallow end's steps.

Anson's alibi on Friday night was tight. The blonde with whom he'd been playing the drinking game, quarters with tequila snake bites, in the cocktail-hour tent. She and other revelers corroborated that he was with them and not anywhere near the house at the time of Kate's murder.

He was free to go but seemed to be waiting for London to be released. Or maybe he was waiting to learn his sister's fate.

Maybe he was hanging around because he didn't have a place to go. Who knew the real story? He certainly didn't seem very devoted to his fiancée.

That is none of my business.

"I can leave anytime I want," London continues as she huffs and scooches her body around on the chaise lounge as if she's having a difficult time getting comfortable. "I mean, he arrested Betsy. He's got the murderer. Why does he still want me to stick around?"

"My sister is not a murderer," Anson says.

"Shut up, Anson," London says. "She's in jail. She did it. She was jealous of Kate replacing her in the wedding. Motive. Means … and … whatever the other word is. She even returned to the scene of the crime."

Anson replaces the cap on the oil, puts it on the table, and stands up. "Yeah, it sounds like you're protesting a little too much. Maybe you're the one who did it."

"Sit down, moron," London says. "You didn't get my legs."

"Do it yourself," he says and walks away.

London huffs again and closes her eyes. "I am so over him."

Judging by Anson's expression, the feeling is mutual.

"Tell your policeman friend I'm leaving tomorrow," she says.

"You might want to talk to Ian before you make plans. If you leave and Chief Bradley needs to question you further, you'll have to come back."

"That's what the phone is for. I mean, if he and the town of Hemlock want to start paying my hotel bill—the hotel manager said they will start billing me tomorrow—then I'd be happy to lie around the pool waiting for him to do his job."

"Okay, London," I say. "I'm sure it will all work out for you, but I need to go into the office for a bit—"

"You can't go to your office," she says. "It's a crime scene."

"I'm working out of my mother's bridal shop."

I stop short of telling her she's not my only client. Other clients are paying me to plan weddings for them.

She raises up on one elbow and squints at me. "Don't go, Jenna."

"I have to, London. I need to get some work done."

"No." She looks panicked.

"London, what's wrong?"

"I need you here."

She pushes herself into a sitting position and covers her stomach with a towel. "Look, I know since the wedding went up in smoke, your business and Gracewood Hall aren't really getting the payoff that you would've if that woman hadn't died."

Now, I'm getting upset. She's saying this as if Kate ruined her wedding on purpose.

"If you stick around, I'll make it worth your while," she says. "I promise."

She's acting like a five-year-old with separation anxiety—or a master manipulator who has no concern for anyone but herself.

I'm sensing the latter.

When I don't answer, she says, "I don't want to be alone."

She sounds afraid. I realize this is the first time she has let her mask slip since she arrived in Hemlock in a swirl of pomp and self-importance.

The bigger part of me feels sorry for her. What is it like to have more than three million followers but not a single true friend?

I stand to leave when my phone sounds a text tone.

My stomach flips when I see Ian's name on the display screen. He's been so busy with London's case that we haven't seen each other since Friday night.

"Hi—have you seen London? I'm trying to reach her, but she's not in her room or answering texts."

"She's with me by the hotel pool."

"I'm in the lobby. I'll be right there."

I lower my body onto the deck chair to wait for him.

"Good, you're staying." London flips over onto her stomach like a flopping fish, settles in, and closes her eyes without another mention of how she'll *make it worth my while* for hanging out.

The best thing she can do for me will be to leave Hemlock. Gracewood Hall remained a crime scene through the weekend, and she's not mentioned rebooking the wedding, which is fine with me. Now that I know what she and her entourage are all about, I'll pass if she suggests setting a redo date.

Being set free from her chaos will be plenty worth my while.

I watch her lying there like a sleeping bear. I don't tell her that Ian is looking for her. I don't know why he needs to see her, but I suspect if I tell her, she will latch onto the worst possible scenario and maybe even bolt before Ian can explain.

It doesn't matter anyway because a moment later, Ian, looking like an ad for men's cologne, in his gray suit with a white shirt and blue tie, emerges through the doors leading from the hotel to the pool. Shading his eyes from the sun, he looks around and waves when he spots us and begins walking toward us.

Again, my stomach flips.

I stifle a sigh.

I really do have it bad for him.

He bought a house in Hemlock and moved here from Asheville to start his own law practice. But when he told the partners of Stanley, Howard, and Cash he was leaving, they offered him a junior partnership. They even gave him access to a corporate apartment in Asheville for those nights when he needed to work late and didn't want to make the forty-five-minute drive back to Hemlock.

It isn't ideal—not for me, at least. But I'm busy with my business, and he seems happy about the promotion. I have to be supportive. At least he hasn't talked about selling the house and moving back to Asheville.

"Hello, ladies," he says.

London raises her head and squints at him.

"Ian. Where did you come from?" she asks.

"I have some news," he says. "Jenna, would you please give us a moment? Or we could always go inside where it's more private. Your choice, London."

London pushes up onto her left elbow. "Will I like this news?"

I take the opportunity to get the heck out of there while I can.

London is in Ian's capable hands.

And, yes, I trust him implicitly.

THE GOOD NEWS is London is officially cleared as a suspect in Kate's murder.

Even though her fingerprints were on the glass of the shattered champagne bottle, there was no blood or tissue on the bottle shards or on London's dress, which is consistent with her story that she had been in shock when she'd discovered Kate's body and had dropped the champagne bottle that she'd been holding.

The bad news is Ian has to go to Los Angeles for a few days to meet with Clint Evans from Evans and Reid, the firm representing London.

It's not *bad* news. Not for him, at least. It's just that we haven't seen much of each other lately. I miss him, and I was hoping to get some Ian time. But what's a few more days?

Hopefully, by the time he gets back, Kate's killer will be behind bars, and we will begin the process of picking up the pieces.

When we talked, he told me something interesting. While the trauma to Kate's skull was probably caused by a similar type of wine or champagne bottle, it's likely the murder weapon was a full, sealed bottle. A full bottle would've delivered a more forceful impact than the half-full open bottle from which London had been drinking.

Plus, he confirmed my theory. If London had hit Kate with the open bottle, she would've had to lift it over her head. That would've caused the champagne to spill onto the bodice of her dress, which the lab found was clean of champagne—and blood and tissue, which would've become airborne upon impact. The lab did find traces of champagne on the skirt of London's dress but concluded they were consistent with a champagne bottle dropping and shattering on the terrazzo floor.

He also told me that Betsy Rutt had been released after her arraignment. Her alibi checked out. The surveillance video from the Hemlock Inn showed her leaving her room when she'd attested, and the Uber driver confirmed her story.

Now, I'm standing in Mom's kitchen, telling her about the day's events while I chop iceberg lettuce and tomatoes for the tacos we're having for dinner.

"If the police have looked at the video and not made any arrests, there's probably nothing on it," Mom says as she stirs the seasoned taco meat she's cooking. "But it wouldn't hurt to give it a look."

"Maybe we can do that tonight," I suggest. "We're only looking for activity around Kate's and Betsy's rooms. Since London and Anson were at Gracewood Hall when everything happened, I don't know that we need to look at their room. It shouldn't take long to view the footage in question."

"Speaking of London and Anson, they didn't waste any time packing," she says.

"I know. They were so eager to get out of here. Ian had to go to the office in Asheville to prepare for his trip to LA tomorrow. So, he offered to drop them off at the airport.

"They didn't even stick around to see what happened with Betsy. For a minute, I thought Anson might stay in Hemlock because, before Ian got to the hotel to tell London she was free to go, Anson was worried about Betsy and seemed like he'd had his fill of London."

I tell her how Anson took issue with London saying Betsy killed Kate.

"They must be on their way to Cabo by now," I continue. "If they weren't, I'm sure London would've called and demanded I pick them up because London Brinks isn't capable of calling an Uber like a regular person."

We laugh.

"Since Jack is preoccupied with the case and Ian will be out of town, you know what we should do?" I ask and cock a brow at her.

"I'm afraid to ask," she says.

"We should go to Greenville, South Carolina, and pay a visit to your good buddy, Greg Paulson, and ask him why he was following Kate."

Mom grimaces. Not the reaction I expected.

"I don't know, Jenna. He's a pretty big guy. And formidable. You didn't see him."

"Then maybe we can swing by and pick up Kate's boyfriend, David, and take him with us?"

"Doesn't David live in Asheville?" Mom asks.

I nod.

"That's not exactly on the way."

"I know." I set down the serrated knife I'd been using to dice the tomatoes and dry my hands on a tea towel. "There's safety in numbers. And I'm sure David has questions about why Greg Paulson was following Kate."

Mom looks dubious. "I'm not sure that's a good idea. We haven't ruled out David as a suspect."

"That's true," I say. "But can you think of a better way to test the waters where he's concerned than to make him think we suspect someone else? He might let his guard down."

Mom shifts from one foot to the other and inhales like she's about to say something, but I preempt her objections by holding out my hand.

"Think about it," I say. "I just … feel like I need to be doing something to help find Kate's killer since I'm the one who asked her to come to Hemlock."

"But putting yourself in harm's way won't solve anything."

"I know, it's just that—" Unexpected tears sting the backs of my eyes, and I choke on my words.

"Oh, honey, I'm sorry." She turns off the burner and pushes the pan onto a cool area of the stove. "I know this is hard on you. We don't know what Kate was involved in. I mean, you said she was jumpy because she was being followed, and Sabrina said the police found a lot of money in her room. People don't carry around that much cash these days. Now that London and Betsy have been cleared, I worry that Kate might've been involved in something bigger and more dangerous than we can handle. Maybe Jack is right. Maybe we should leave this one to the police. Let's sit down and talk about it."

She guides me to the kitchen table and pulls out a chair for me. I sit and bury my face in my hands.

She rubs my back for a moment, the way she used to do when I was young and thought my world was ending for whatever childish reason.

"How about a glass of water?" she offers.

I nod, and a sob wracks my body.

She fills a tumbler and says, "I'm of two minds about this whole thing. Part of me wants to lock the doors and stay inside until Jack figures out what's going on, but the other part wants to get in the car, go to Greenville, and confront Paulson about why he was following Kate. We can't do anything tonight. Let's sleep on it. In the meantime, why don't we do something fun?"

I wave away the suggestion, suddenly exhausted. "I don't feel like doing anything. I might call it an early evening."

"I would love to do something fun," Gigi says as she sashays into the kitchen, fresh from her nap. "I slept much longer than I planned, but I feel so rested and refreshed that I'm absolutely game for some fun. What did you have in mind?"

"I was thinking that we could set up an official murder board," Mom says. "I have my notes, but they're starting to get unwieldy. It's always easier to see the connections when you have it all laid out in front of you."

"Oh, dear." Gigi clutches the collar of her cobalt-blue blouse. "A murder board? That sounds so savage. But it also sounds thrilling. Count me in. What do we do?"

I don't want Gigi to see that I've been crying. It will upset her. Keeping my back to her, I chop onion for fresh pico de gallo to accompany the tacos.

Now, I can blame my red eyes on the onion fumes.

"That's how Jenna and I have made progress when we've

looked into crimes in the past," I say. "Right, Jenna?"

"Uhh-huh," I answer.

"As of today, we can officially mark two previous persons of interest off our list."

She explained that Ian had said London and Anson were officially cleared today.

"By some miracle, Jenna was able to keep London far away from Gracewood Hall and the curious crowd that's gathered outside the house's gates."

"Who else goes on this murder board?" Gigi asks.

"All the people who might've had the means, motive, and opportunity to kill Kate need to be on the board," I say, feeling better at the thought of doing something productive like that.

I glance over my shoulder and see Gigi pull a face. "Are you sure London and her fiancé are cleared? I don't trust either of them."

"Anson has a solid alibi, and the crime lab said London's clothing did not show evidence that she murdered Kate," I say. "They left today to take their honeymoon trip."

"Honeymoon?" Gigi shakes her head. "They're not even married. Not to mention, who goes on a honeymoon trip after a woman in their bridal party was killed? If you ask me, there's something very fishy about those two. I don't care if they were cleared. Let's put them on the board even if we have to cross them off temporarily … you never know about people. Who else?"

"There's Greg Paulson, who was purportedly following Kate," Mom says as she sets the bowls of taco fixings on the table.

"What about Betsy, the bridesmaid who broke into Gracewood Hall after London fired her? Is she still in jail?"

We tell her Betsy was released after her arraignment. Her alibi checked out, and the surveillance video confirmed her story.

"I suppose if the police have cleared her, we shouldn't press charges," Gigi says. "But let's put her on the board anyway. And let's put Kate's boyfriend, David, up there, too. I think he's innocent, but have we really looked into him?"

"I knew him in college, but I must admit, I don't know him well. He was definitely in Kate's orbit—then and now. So, yes, he can be on the board. Who else, Mom?"

I set the pico on the table, and we all sit down to dinner.

"We need to think beyond the obvious," Mom says. "Who were Kate's enemies, and why would she have an envelope containing twenty thousand cash in her hotel room?"

The three of us stare blankly at each other.

"We really don't know much about Kate, do we?" Mom says.

"I hate to say it, but no, we don't."

"We need to find out," Mom says. "I've had a minute to think about it, and I agree that we need to pay a visit to both David Martin and Greg Paulson."

Chapter Nine
~ Maddie ~

AFTER SPENDING THE better part of Monday night fast-forwarding through the Hemlock Inn surveillance video, we found nothing interesting.

Jenna had called Sabrina, and she'd given us Kate's room number after we made a hand-to-God vow that we wouldn't tell anyone. As it turns out, we'll be able to keep that promise easily because the video didn't show much we didn't already know.

We saw Kate entering her room after checking in on Friday morning. She returned later that afternoon to get ready for the rehearsal dinner. The curious thing was that the time stamp showed her returning to her room more than forty-five minutes after leaving Gracewood Hall. It only takes fifteen minutes to drive from the venue to the hotel.

Finally, we saw her leave in her beautiful shimmery dress, unaware that each step she took was leading her closer to her death less than an hour later.

It gives me shivers. She had no idea a figurative clock was

counting down her last minutes. With each step she took, she was moving closer to the end of her life.

There's no sign of David coming and going from the hotel, which is one of the reasons we decide to visit him first.

We'll pay a condolence call and convince him to accompany us when we visit Greg Paulson.

I've never been good at making condolence calls—or receiving them, for that matter.

After I received official word from the navy that Frank's remains had been found and identified, so many people showed up to pay their respects and bring food I had to shift into automatic pilot mode to get through.

However, after the numbness wore off and reality set in that Frank was gone, it was comforting knowing that I had a support system in my friends and neighbors. I mean, I've always had community support, even when Frank was alive, but he was stationed away from us. However, once the official word came down confirming Frank's death, it was as if the entire town, which had held out hope for his coming home someday right alongside me, went into mourning with me.

Even though David Martin lives in Asheville and we're not exactly neighbors, making a condolence call feels necessary. Plus, if anyone might know why Greg Paulson was following Kate, it will be David.

Jenna and I pile into my RAV4 and head to Asheville. Since I've already come face-to-face with Greg Paulson in the

Hemlock Inn parking lot, I have an idea of what we are dealing with. He is an intimidating guy, and he might be Kate's killer.

We can handle ourselves, but we need to be safe. If we can convince David to go with us when we visit Paulson, all the better.

Finding David's phone number and business address is easier than I thought. He works as an independent investment banker/stockbroker, and his contact information is on his website. Jenna called him, and he invited us to lunch.

"There's a parking place." Jenna points at a green car pulling out of a space a short walk to the restaurant, which specializes in tapas. I flip on my blinker and pull in.

David is waiting at a table near the front door inside the restaurant. He acknowledges us with a lifted chin and stands.

He hugs us one at a time when we get to the table.

"You smell good," Jenna says. "What cologne are you wearing? I might get some for my boyfriend."

David smiles devilishly, suggesting he's willing to flirt if she is. "It's called *Acqua Di Parma*. I've worn it for years. In fact, Kate's the one who turned me onto it back in the day. She gave me a bottle for our first Christmas together."

He looks down at his feet and nods as if reliving the bittersweet memory. His eyes fill with tears, and he shakes his head.

Jenna and I murmur our condolences.

He smiles, though it's clear to see that he is heartbroken.

"But, hey, thanks for coming all this way to meet me," he says. "It's nice to spend time with someone who knew Kate. We hadn't been back together very long. We both worked so much that we spent what little free time we had together. I didn't have a chance to get to know her friends very well. Talking about her with you helps more than you know."

I feel a little guilty that I want to delve into the investigation more than I want to talk about Kate, but hearing what he says might help us discover another avenue to investigate.

David and Jenna bittersweetly reminisce about their college years and time spent with Kate when the server approaches and takes our drink order. This seems to pull them back to the present.

The restaurant features small plates. The server suggests that we each select two and share. With our orders out of the way, I grab the opportunity to ask, "Do you have any idea who might have wanted to hurt Kate?"

David's mouth flattens into a line. He plays with the paper wrapper that covers the straw before looking back at me.

"The police asked me the same thing."

Bingo.

So, the police have talked to him. That's part one of an essential two-part question I want to cross off my list before we leave the restaurant.

Now, for part two.

"Who interviewed you?" I ask. "Asheville or Hemlock

police?"

"Both. Someone from the Asheville police was there, but the guy who asked the questions was from Hemlock. I think his last name was Bradley?"

Jenna and I lock gazes.

"Do you know him?" David asks.

"I do know the chief," I say. "Hemlock is a small town. Everyone knows everyone. What did he ask you?"

David shrugs. "You know, general, run-of-the-mill investigative questions. Where were you when the murder occurred?"

Jenna jumps in. "Yeah, I was surprised you didn't accompany Kate to the wedding. It would've been perfectly fine for you to be her plus-one."

"I wanted to, but I had some unexpected work come up. A new client who needs a lot of handholding wanted me to review some things—" He presses his lips together.

His throat works as he swallows. He closes his eyes and shakes his head.

"I keep asking myself what would've happened if I'd told the client I was out of town and I'd help her on Monday. Maybe if I'd gone to the wedding with Kate, she'd still be … still be…" A sob stifles his words.

"Will you excuse me for a moment, please?" he asks and leaves the table amidst a chorus of our *of course* and *absolutely*.

After he's out of earshot, Jenna whistles under her

breath. "This is harder than I thought it would be."

"I know. We should've figured it would be difficult. The guy's girlfriend was murdered not even a week ago."

After a few moments, David returns to the table. His eyes are red.

"Sorry about that," he says. "Grief is a weird thing. When I think I can hold it together, it sneaks up from behind and pulls the rug out from under me."

"No apology necessary," I say. "We get it. I'm a widow. Jenna lost her father. It takes time. You must be kind to yourself and give yourself the grace to grieve."

He stares at his hands and nods. His eyes look a little glassy, like he's here, but not completely.

"David, I feel like I owe it to you to be upfront with you," I say. "Jenna and I are looking into Kate's murder ourselves."

His brows knit, and he looks alarmed.

"Why would you do that?"

"Since Kate was a friend of Jenna's and it happened at Gracewood Hall," I say. "It feels personal. Plus, I don't know if you know this, but I write a cozy mystery series. Investigating crime is second nature."

"But this is real life," he says. "There's a killer on the loose. It could be dangerous. Not that you're not perfectly capable of taking care of yourselves, but wouldn't it be a lot safer if you left the investigating to the police?"

Of course, it will, but I don't want to get into the ups

and downs of my relationship with Jack or how this case feels even more personal because Jack insisted that I butt out.

Instead of trying to explain, I opt for, "I've never been one to play it safe."

A slight smile turns up the corners of David's mouth, but it doesn't quite reach his eyes. "In that case, I have some investments I'd love to talk to you about."

He says it with such a straight face that it takes a beat before I realize he's cracking a joke.

"Mom, he's kidding," Jenna says.

David turns up his palms. "I am. Unless you're in the market to invest. I'm a stockbroker."

The three of us laugh.

I shake my head.

"I'm sure investments are the last thing on your mind today," he says. "I get it. They're not really on my mind either, and that's what I do. All I can think about is that I want to make sure whoever did this to Kate is caught and put behind bars. Because of that, count me in on the investigation. I'll help you in any way I can."

"Good," Jenna says. "Would you be willing to answer a few questions?"

He places his forearms on the table and leans forward. "Ask me anything."

"Did the police verify your alibi for the time that Kate was killed?" I ask.

He nods solemnly. "They did."

"Where were you?" Jenna asks.

"I was with the client I mentioned earlier. The one who pulled me away from the wedding."

"Can you give us the client's name?" I ask.

David opens his mouth but then shuts it again. He looks torn.

"I don't think so, Maddie. The police have already contacted her. I hope you can understand that it puts me in a precarious position. I've already shared more of my personal life with this client than I normally would."

Jenna and I remain quiet. David shifts and exhales through his nose.

"Okay, her name is Dana Coleman. I'll give you her contact information." David picks up his phone and pulls up the address book. His cellphone is tipped toward me, and I can see the name Dana Coleman in the header, but the phone number is farther down on the page.

"Look, this woman is a new client. She was unnerved by the police contacting her. The last thing people want is for the police to ask questions about their financial advisor. I fear I'll lose her business if you come around and start asking questions."

He shrugs. "But it's up to you. Here's her number."

David types, and a few seconds later, my phone sounds a text tone alert, and David's text pops up.

"I won't contact her," I say. "I'm sure if your alibi hadn't checked out and the police had any doubts, you wouldn't be sitting here with us right now."

"You're right," he says. "That's a good point, but if you change your mind and decide to contact her, you have her number."

"If I do, I'll let you know before I call her so you can do any damage control you need to."

"Thanks for understanding," David says.

The server shows up with our food. It's the perfect transition away from the awkwardness of the Dana Coleman situation.

The food looks delicious and smells heavenly. We ordered a charcuterie board, an eggplant dish served with roasted red peppers and a crusty baguette, sauteed shrimp in a sherry broth, and a tapas-sized portion of paella, among other things.

My stomach growls in appreciation of the feast before us, reminding me I'm famished.

Before the server walks away, David asks, "Are you sure you don't want some sangria? It pairs perfectly with what we ordered."

"Go ahead," I say to Jenna. "But none for me because I have to drive."

The two of them split a small pitcher of the restaurant's famous white sangria, which features an added kick of triple sec and brandy mixed in with the wine.

After we've filled our plates and *oohed* and *ahhed* over how delicious everything tastes, Jenna says, "David, you mentioned that you don't know Kate's friends very well, but does she have any family? I think I told you, and she might've mentioned it. We had classes together, but I didn't know much about her personal life."

He swallows the bite he'd been chewing. "Sadly, both of her parents have passed, but she has a sister who lives in Savannah."

I remember Sabrina mentioning that Kate's sister was coming to collect her belongings. I wish I knew when she would be in Hemlock so I could talk to her.

"Unfortunately, she and Ruth, that's her sister's name, are estranged." He shrugs. "Other than Ruth, I don't know of any family."

He sets his fork down. "When I called Ruth with the bad news, I offered to plan Kate's memorial service, but she refused."

"That's so sad," Jenna says. "So, you talked to Ruth?"

"Yes, I felt the news would be better coming from me rather than the police."

"How did it go?" I ask.

David grimaces. "I need to be honest with you about something. When we were in college, I dated Ruth casually before I met Kate. When Ruth introduced me to Kate, it was love at first sight. As I said, Ruth and I were seeing each other casually, but when Kate and I told her we were involved, she went ballistic. She said she wanted nothing to do with either of us."

Jenna squints at David. "I never met Ruth at school."

"She was a couple of years older than Kate. You and Kate had classes together junior and senior year, right?"

Jenna nods. "I guess by that time, Ruth had graduated. Kate never mentioned her. So, they remained estranged even though the two of you broke up?"

"Ruth is one of the reasons Kate broke up with me," David says. "She said she needed to try and make amends with her sister. It never happened. There was a lot of rivalry between them. You know how Kate is … smart, beautiful. Things always seem to go easily for her—" David's voice breaks. "Sometimes I forget she's … not here anymore."

"I know," Jenna says. "She was always so full of life. It doesn't seem possible that she's gone. I didn't realize she was the one who broke up with you. I thought it was the other way around. She was so distraught when it happened that she disappeared for a few days. I thought we'd fail our marketing project. We were partners, but she showed up at the last minute, and we pulled off an *A* on the project."

"That sounds just like Kate." David's lips curve into a melancholy smile. "She was always trying to make everyone happy. We were in love, but she thought the only way she could get back into her sister's good graces was to break up with me."

"Things like this make me glad I'm an only child. It's been what? Nine years since that happened, and Ruth could never let it go?"

David shakes his head. "It's crazy. She told me that Kate was so self-absorbed, wanting to get ahead at all costs, that she knew her sister would cross the wrong person someday."

Jenna and I flinch. We look at each other and then back at David in horror.

"That's what she said in response to the news that her sister was murdered?" Jenna asks. "That basically, she had it coming? Did you tell this to the police?"

"I did. They assured me they would follow up."

I make a mental note that Ruth lives in Savannah.

"David, would you please share Ruth's contact information with us?"

"I found her online, but I didn't save her number. She's married now—she goes by Ruth Asher Long—and wasn't thrilled to hear from me. Maybe that barb about crossing the wrong person was more for my benefit than a true sentiment about her sister."

"No matter how you look at it, it's weird," I say. "It wasn't as if you were making a social call. Do you think Ruth might've been angry or resentful enough at Kate to kill her? Especially since the two of you had gotten back together?"

David blinks as if the thought hasn't occurred to him. He blows an audible breath out. "That's hard to say. There's certainly no love lost between them."

"David, are you familiar with a man named Greg Paulson?" Jenna asks.

His eyes narrow, and the color of his face deepens.

He murmurs a choice word that seems out of character for him. "Yep. I know Paulson. Why do you ask?"

"We think he was following Kate right before her death," Jenna says.

"The sorry son of a—" David snaps his mouth shut, trapping the word. "He's a PI my ex-girlfriend hired to follow Kate and me. I thought I'd made it clear to him that he needed to leave us alone, or I would file a restraining order."

I have to make a conscious effort to keep my mouth from falling open. I have so many questions, but Jenna beats me to the most obvious one.

"Your ex-girlfriend hired a PI to follow you and Kate?"

David pushes his plate away, props his elbows on the table, and rests his head in his hands. "Why didn't I see this before now?"

"See what, David?" I ask. "Do you think your ex—what's her name?"

He looks up. His eyes are red and weary. "Her name is Tilly. Tilly Franklin, and she's a..." His words trail off. "I know this will sound harsh, but I believe she's mentally unstable. After we broke up, I had to get a restraining order to make her leave me alone. When I started seeing Kate again, she hired Paulson to follow us. Oh, my g..." He rests his head in his hands again.

"Did you tell this to the police?" Jenna asks.

David shakes his head. "It's been so much so fast. It

hasn't even been a week, and I haven't had time to come to terms with everything. Much less think straight. I've been losing myself in my work. If I don't, it feels like I'll drown in the grief. But I will tell them. As soon as I get back to the office, I'll call Chief Bradley. Because I think Tilly might be the person who killed Kate."

I hold up my hand. "Wait, so Chief Bradley didn't ask you about Paulson?"

David shakes his head.

I gave Jack the information. Had he not believed me? Had he not thought it a credible enough lead to ask someone to run the tags? Or maybe he hasn't had time to draw a line from Paulson to David.

Though, that seems unlikely.

The only reason Jack wouldn't have asked David about the guy who'd been following his girlfriend was if he didn't have the information when he talked to David.

Resentment roils in my belly. I try to ignore it by turning my focus back to David.

"When exactly did Chief Bradley talk to you?" I ask.

"Late Friday night, maybe even early Saturday morning. He woke me up, so it was the wee hours."

"You were home?" Jenna asks.

David nods. "I drove back to Asheville around five after Kate returned to Gracewood Hall. I met my client, Dana Coleman, for dinner around six-forty-five."

"Where did you have dinner?"

"We went to a place called Twisted Laurel. It's not too far from here. We had a bite and a couple of beers. I was home before ten. The next thing I knew, the police were knocking on my door telling me that Kate was dead. I have to talk to the police again. I have to let them know about Paulson and Tilly."

Jenna slants me a glance, and I know she's thinking the same thing I am.

If Jack doesn't know about the ex-girlfriend hiring Paulson—that probably means Jack has been too pigheaded to follow up on the information about the silver Honda that I had provided—which admittedly is out of character for him because, usually, he is so thorough … and levelheaded, but right now that's beside the point. If Jack hasn't followed up and I know something that he doesn't know because I talked to someone who was not a suspect, technically, I'm not interfering in the case.

That also means I need to find out as much information as possible about Tilly Franklin before David officially reports her to the police.

"David, I know this is difficult to talk about, but can you tell us more about Tilly?" I ask in a soothing voice.

He looks up at the ceiling, and for a moment, I'm afraid he'll refuse, but then he nods. "Originally, Tilly was my client. She's pretty and outgoing. And more than a bit obsessive. She'd come into an inheritance and wanted help investing it. I learned later that she was also spoiled to the point that she always had to get her way. She wouldn't take no for an answer when she decided that the two of us were meant to be. I told her I couldn't be her financial advisor if we dated. It wasn't ethical. So, she fired me and started pursuing me relentlessly. I must confess, I buckled under the pressure and started seeing her.

"She and I had only been dating for a couple of weeks when she decided we were getting married. She proposed to me and even started wearing a diamond engagement ring. She said it was a family heirloom. It's the size of a headlight. Even though I told her it was too soon, she said I would come around, and she started planning our wedding.

"A mutual friend recently told me she's still wearing the ring even though we haven't seen each other in months." He shakes his head. "One of the first red flags should've been that she didn't have any close friends, so she hired someone to be her maid of honor."

Jenna and I gasp.

David gives us a knowing look. "It was Kate. After all these years, she was back in my life, and just like the first time I saw her, it hit me like a thunderbolt. Only this time, I had to believe it was a sign that it was meant to be, that we were supposed to get back together. And believe me, I don't give much credence to signs and woo-woo nonsense. But this … this was different. This was Kate. She was back like a gift from God.

"I wasn't in love with Tilly. I had never been. After she

became so fixated on getting married, I knew I had to end it with her, but I wanted to let her down easily. I worked a lot and put some distance between us, hoping she would lose interest, but then Kate came into the picture.

"As far as I was concerned, it was the end of the line for Tilly and me. Kate was a little more cautious. She told me she'd never stopped loving me and wanted to be together but asked me to give it enough time to seem respectable after my breaking up with Tilly."

He pins us with another knowing look.

"It was clear Tilly was a bit unbalanced. Kate was concerned about her business and how it would look to other clients if the hired maid of honor ran away with the groom. So, I ended it with Tilly. Kate and I kept everything on the down-low, meeting in private, and trying to be as discreet as possible.

"Tilly hadn't accepted that our relationship was over. She hired Greg Paulson, who started following us. She even confronted us one night when I went to Kate's place. We had to call the police and get a restraining order. But that was more than a year ago.

"After we took legal steps, Tilly kept her distance. I thought she'd found someone else or at least had gotten over the fact that Kate and I were in love and wanted to make a life together. Actually, I rarely even thought of Tilly, which is why it didn't even enter my mind that she might be responsible for Kate's death until you mentioned Greg Paulson."

The three of us sit there in silence.

I finally ask, "David, do you think Tilly is capable of murder?"

His brows knit as he stares into the middle distance as if weighing the possibility. "That's not for me to say. I mean, do I think she's capable? Maybe. Do I think she did it?" He holds up his hands. "I don't feel right passing judgment on her without knowing if she has an alibi for Friday night."

He's right. I know nothing about Tilly Franklin except what David has told me. While this doesn't paint a flattering picture of her, it's incomplete information.

"Would you share Tilly's contact information with us?" Jenna asks. "Then we can get in touch with her and ask."

David shakes his head. "I don't have it anymore. After the restraining order, I blocked her number and deleted her contact information from my phone. I figured it was the best thing to do in case she tried falsely coming after me. Since her number was programmed into my phone, I never learned it."

"You must know her address," Jenna presses.

"I do, but we need to leave this to the police. She's dangerous." He looks at his watch. "I'm leaving for Raleigh tonight because I have an early morning meeting with a client tomorrow. I want to talk to the police before I leave, which means I need to go." He catches our server's eye and makes a scribbling motion in midair.

"I'm sorry to leave before we finish the meal, but time

will be tight."

"You barely ate anything, David," I say. "I can get the check."

"Nonsense," he says. "Since you came all this way, lunch is on me. I hope you two will stay and enjoy it."

We thanked him, and a few moments later, as soon as he left the restaurant, Jenna took out her phone.

"It's too late for us to go to Greenville today, but I'm texting Finster to see if she can dig up contact information for Tilly Franklin in Asheville and Ruth Asher Long in Savannah."

Chapter Ten

~ Jenna ~

I OWE FINSTER big time.

I don't know how she does it, and frankly, I don't want to know, but she came through big time, supplying contact information for Ruth and Tilly.

Since Ruth Asher Long and Tilly—short for Matilda—Franklin aren't common names, I figured it wouldn't be as difficult as asking her to trace the silver Honda, but since this request came on the heels of the silver Honda search, it felt like a big ask.

I'll make it up to her somehow. Though I don't know exactly what I'd be able to do since I doubt she'll need anything in my line of work in the near future, but you never know.

We decided to pay a visit to Tilly Franklin first.

She lives in Ashville's Montford neighborhood, which is famous for its tree-lined streets, gentrified historic homes, and perfectly manicured lawns.

Mom parks the car on the street in front of the address

Finster gave us.

The house is lovely, especially for a thirty-two-year-old. Certainly, more home than I can afford right now, but I guess that's one of the benefits of a trust fund. Also, according to Finster, Tilly is vice president of media relations for CarolinaVantage Industries, the company her family owned before it went public. Tilly and her family hold a majority interest.

She earns a decent salary and can afford several houses like this or better.

The front door of the gray arts and crafts bungalow is painted deep cranberry. It sports a polished brass pineapple door knocker and kickplate. A deep, welcoming front porch, complete with hanging potted ferns, white wicker rocking chairs, and a daybed swing laden with decorative pillows, spans the length of the front of the house. My gaze keeps wandering back to the daybed swing. It seems to be calling to me after the glass of sangria I drank with lunch.

"Nice place," I say. "We can only hope that Tilly will be as welcoming as her home's curb appeal."

"That's the truth," Mom says as she gazes at the house through the driver's side window. "But I have a question. If Tilly Franklin lives in Asheville, why did she hire a private investigator based out of Greenville, South Carolina? It's only about an hour away, but you'd think that a city like Asheville would have plenty of PIs that could help her."

"That's a good question," I say. "I'll add it to the list of questions."

"Have you been making a list?" Mom asks.

"Not yet," I say. "But it might be a good idea to start so that we're prepared. Speaking of being prepared, how did you want to handle this?"

We spend a few minutes coming up with a plan.

"Now, I suppose we need to knock on her door."

I think about how David had to take out a restraining order to stop Tilly's unwanted advances. The lovely house seems at odds with a person who would badger her ex to the point of legal action. Though, I don't know where I expected Tilly to live.

"We might as well get this over with," Mom says. "Iris has been so good about caring for Aggie and Homie, I'm starting to feel bad. I need to get home as soon as possible."

Knowing my mother, it's not so much that she feels like she's imposing as she misses her dogs. They're like her children, and she hates to be away from them for too long, especially when she's dealing with something unpleasant, like having second thoughts about her engagement... and murder. The dogs are her woobies, her emotional support animals.

That's how I know everything is getting to her.

She starts to open her car door, and I say, "Wait a second. I understand why you don't want to tell Jack we're here, but we should tell someone. I'll text Tess the address and let her know what we're doing."

"That's a good idea," Mom says.

I pull my phone from my bag, text the information, and tell her I'll text her after we're done.

Tess answers, *"Should I be worried about you two? Wait, don't answer that. Just be safe."*

With that, we get out of the car and knock on Tilly Franklin's front door.

A tall, thin woman with flawless ivory skin, copper hair, and celadon eyes answers the door. She's not a traditional beauty, but she's striking with her shoulder-length hair pulled back from her face with a pearl-studded headband. The floral Lilly Pulitzer shift dress she's wearing looks crisp and effortlessly cool—not cool as in hip-cool, but casual and unbothered, from the top of her shiny red hair to the bottom of her hot-pink-painted bare toes.

"May I help you?" she asks.

She crosses her arms over the front of her, and I don't know where to look first—at the headlight-sized solitaire on her left ring finger—the engagement ring David had mentioned—or the thick gold rope bracelet on her right wrist.

My stomach drops and rebounds at the sight of it.

It looks an awful lot like the bracelet London gave Kate to wear during the wedding.

The one Kate was wearing the night she died. I have no idea if it was on her body when the coroner took her away.

I glance at Mom to see if she's noticed it, but her gaze is trained on Tilly.

"Hi, are you Tilly Franklin?" Mom asks.

"Yes, I am," Tilly says cautiously.

"I'm Madeliene Bell of Blissful Beginnings Bridal Boutique. Congratulations on your engagement. This must be a very exciting time in your life."

Tilly nods but looks skeptical.

"I have good news for you," Mom says. "I'm so pleased to tell you that you've won the grand prize in the Blissful Beginnings Bridal Boutique sweepstakes."

Yep. She sees it. Or at least the engagement ring because she's going completely rogue on the story that we'd concocted to gain Tilly's trust so she'd invite us in.

As I stare at the bracelet, my mind is spinning, and I can't quite remember the original story. Maybe it's because this one sounds so much better. Because of the London fiasco, Mom has given away a lot of freebies, but if Tilly Franklin murdered Kate, I'd say that's grounds for disqualification from claiming the prizes.

"There must be a mistake. I didn't enter a contest," Tilly says.

"It doesn't matter who entered your name," Mom says, her voice a little too bright. "You're the winner."

From this vantage point, the bracelet simply looks like a plain gold rope, which is a coincidence enough—that the woman who was so jealous of the woman David dumped her for that she would hire a private investigator to follow them—is wearing a bracelet that looks a lot like the one that

Kate was wearing the night she was murdered—but I need to see the other side.

"That's a gorgeous bracelet," I say, but I'm cut short by a familiar male voice.

"Well, well, what are we up to today, ladies?"

"Oh, no," Mom says under her breath.

I don't have to turn around to know at least one of Hemlock's finest is standing behind us.

Mom does turn around. "Chief Bradley and Deputy Salisbury, what a surprise. I was here sharing the good news that Ms. Franklin is the grand prize winner in the Blissful Beginnings Bridal Boutique sweepstakes."

Jack grunts. "Is that so?"

I lock eyes with Jeff, and he sheepishly looks away, like a kid who knows another kid is in big trouble.

Mom and I nod so vigorously that I'll bet we look like a couple of souped-up bobbleheads.

Especially in contrast to Jack, who looks M. A. D. and Jeff, who looks like he wants to be anywhere else but here.

"That will have to wait. We need to speak to Ms. Franklin." He turns to Tilly. "Are you Matilda Franklin?"

"I am."

"Good. I'm Chief Jackson Bradley of the Hemlock, North Carolina, police department. This is my deputy, Jeff Salisbury." When Jack hands her his badge, Tilly moves her arm, and the bracelet turns, revealing the pavé diamond-encrusted letters L and A that have been artfully woven together to look like a heart.

Tilly Franklin is wearing Kate Asher's bracelet.

~ Maddie ~

"What did I just see back there?" I ask as we walk to the car.

"If you're asking what I think you're asking, you saw Tilly Franklin wearing the bracelet that Kate wore the night she died."

My head is spinning with a mix of how mad Jack looked and that we may have just discovered an irrefutable clue. I feel like I'm caught in one of those dreams where I want to run, but my legs won't work.

Even though I can't feel my feet, I make it to the car. Once we're both safe inside, I say, "Does that mean we have proof that Tilly killed Kate?"

"Well, it's bad optics," Jenna says. "I would imagine getting caught wearing the dead woman's bracelet would make her a pretty compelling suspect."

I shiver as I recall the sociopathic picture David had painted of Tilly.

"I have to tell Jack." I take out my phone and fire off a text to him. My hands are shaking so badly that it takes me three tries to get the message right.

"I need to talk to you ASAP. Please don't wait until you're

finished talking to Tilly. Go someplace private and call me. NOW!"

I stare at my phone, waiting for the bubbles to dance, indicating that he's answering me, but I get nothing. "I'm going up there and knocking on the door."

My fingers are on the car door handle, but Jenna stops me with a hand on my arm. "Do you think that's a good idea?"

"I don't care if it is or not. Jack and Jeff are in there with a murderer. They could be in danger. They need to know about the bracelet so they can do something about it before she gets away."

I don't wait for my daughter's response. I get out of the car.

She follows me. Race walking to catch up.

I pound on the door until Tilly answers. Jack and Jeff are standing behind her as if she needs protection from a crazy woman. Boy, do they have it wrong.

"Jack, I need to talk to you right now."

He looks at me like I'm not dealing with a full deck. "Maddie. Go home. We'll talk later."

At a loss for what else to do, I pull my phone from my jeans pocket and try to type in the text field. *Tilly is wearing Kate's bracelet. I think she murdered Kate.*

Maybe I could show it to him without her seeing it.

Again, my hands are shaking so badly that I keep typing the words wrong. Before I finish, Jack tells Jeff, "Will you…"

He doesn't finish the sentence.

I look up in time to see him incline his head toward me and then disappear inside with Tilly.

Jeff steps outside onto the porch and closes the door behind himself.

"Maddie." His voice is pacifying, like he's been asked to deal with someone else's unruly kid and is trying to remain the good guy.

The fact that Jack—the man I'm planning on spending the rest of my life with—discounted me and walked away when I had something important—No. Something that might be a matter of life or death to tell him.

Go home. I will talk to you later.

Sure, Dad. Am I grounded?

"Maddie, you can't be here."

"Well, you know what, Jeff, I am. And the last I checked, it was a free country, and I'm not trespassing. I have one thing to say and then I'll go."

Jeff grimaces. "Well, the trespassing part is debatable. This is private property.

"Look, I know Jack was a little gruff a minute ago, but the mayor is breathing down everyone's neck saying we have to make an arrest in this case. So, Jack's dealing with that pressure on top of the anniversary of Carla's death. And you know how he gets."

"Wait. What?" I say.

"Yeah, you know how he is," Jeff says. "He always gets

down around the time that she was killed. It's hard losing someone you love."

"Yeah, I know."

Jeff rakes his hand through his curly blond hair and grimaces again. "Ugh. Sorry about that, Maddie. Of course, you understand how it is on account of losing Frank." He shrugs. "I didn't mean to be insensitive. We need to cut the chief some slack. You know, give him some space. Everyone at the station walks on eggshells around him this time of year."

So, everyone at the station knows it's the anniversary of Carla's death.

I didn't know because he's never shared that information with me.

All I know is that Carla was a cop, and she was killed in the line of duty when they lived in Orlando. That's why he moved here. And I learned all of that from the gossip brigade.

Jack didn't tell me.

Whenever I've tried to get him to open up about his late wife and his life before he moved to Hemlock, a wall goes up.

He shuts me out.

Clearly, the subject isn't taboo for everyone.

Not if the entire Hemlock police force knows that this is the anniversary of Carla's death.

Suddenly, it feels as if something inside of me is cracking

into a million tiny, irreparable pieces that I'll never be able to put back together.

I didn't realize it until now, but this is why I think neither of us is ready to get married again.

"You're right, Jeff. I need to give him some room."

I glance at Jenna, who is staring at me with wide, sympathetic eyes. Then I head toward the car.

"Hey, Maddie, you said you had something to tell me?"

I stop with my hand on the car door. Tears are already rolling down my cheeks. I can't turn around and look at Jeff because I don't want him to see me like this. So, I say without looking back, "Ask Tilly Franklin where she got the bracelet she's wearing."

ABOUT AN HOUR later, my phone rings as I'm turning into the driveway.

It's hooked up to the car's navigation system. So, the automated attendant announces that Jackson Bradley is calling.

"Are you going to answer that?" Jenna asks.

I let it sail to voicemail.

I forgot that the auto attendant will automatically play the message as soon as it's recorded. Now, Jack's voice is sounding through my car speakers.

I rest my head on my hands, which grip the steering wheel at the twelve o'clock position.

"Maddie. It's Jack."

I swallow hard. His words are terse and measured. He's furious.

"Why were you at Tilly Franklin's house? Look, David told me he had lunch with you and Jenna today. He said he told you about Matilda Franklin. I don't know how much clearer I can say this, but you have to stay out of this investigation. This isn't one of your books. It's murder. This is real, and it's dangerous."

Then he hangs up without asking me to call him back. He doesn't even ask if we can discuss it.

He said his piece and made it clear that was the end of it.

"Are you okay?" Jenna asks.

"I'm fine."

Or at least I would be if things could return to how they used to be rather than crumbling around me.

~ Maddie ~

A FEW NIGHTS later, Ian is home from California and asks Jenna out for dinner.

At first, she didn't want to go because I still hadn't heard from Jack after the fiasco at Tilly Franklin's house. Of course, the line of communication runs both ways. I haven't tried to see him either. Instead, I've taken Jeff's advice to heart, and I'm giving Jack some room.

Because of that, I told my daughter there is no sense in staying home with me when she can be out having a good time.

Gigi and I will be fine.

Plus, Ian had made a reservation at Chez Paris. I told her if she didn't go, I would.

It made us both smile.

But I wasn't smiling for long.

About an hour after she left, Jack knocked on my front door.

All I had to do was look at his face to know that this wouldn't start or end well.

Gigi must've sensed it, too, because after saying a quick hello to Jack, she went into her bedroom and shut the door.

"Come in and sit down," I say. "Would you like something to drink?"

"Thanks, no," he says and settles himself on the edge of the sofa.

Homie leans against his leg. Jack reaches down and scratches the dog's ears as the weighted silence stretches between us.

Finally, he asks, "Why didn't you return my call?"

Aggie jumps up and settles in my lap. "You didn't ask me to call you back."

"I didn't realize you needed an invitation," he says.

As we sit in silence, I turn words over in my head, searching for the right thing to say.

But there is no right way to say it.

"Why didn't you tell me it was the anniversary of Carla's death?"

He flinches.

"It's not exactly something I talk about."

"You don't like to talk about it with me, but everyone else seems to know."

He shrugs and stares at a point over my shoulder.

He's clamming up again. Lately, it seems like he has two speeds. Telling me what to do or telling me nothing.

Clearly, if we're going to have this conversation, I need to be direct. "Why won't you talk to me about her, Jack?"

"What's the point?" he asks.

"How can we have a life together if you won't share the things that bother you with me?"

He opens his mouth to say something but closes it again. "Look, I'm just stressed. I don't mean to take things out on you."

He's changing the subject.

"Mayor Dobbins is on my back about catching Kate Asher's killer." He holds up his hands and shakes his head. "I didn't come here to fight with you or talk about this, but since we're on the subject, you need to know I'm under the mayor's microscope. That's why you can't get in the middle of this investigation, Maddie."

"Well, you have to admit, my getting in the middle of things helped you—or at least I tried to help, but you wouldn't even give me thirty seconds of your time." I don't mean for the words to sound as accusatory as they come out. I take care to soften my tone. "Did Jeff tell you to ask Tilly Franklin about the bracelet she was wearing?"

"He asked her about it, and she said David Martin gave it to her."

"Wait a minute. You didn't believe her, did you? Kate Asher was wearing that bracelet the night she was murdered. David Martin has an airtight alibi. That should be enough to arrest Tilly because how else would she have gotten the bracelet?"

"That bracelet was not among Kate Asher's possessions that were logged in at the morgue."

"Of course, it wasn't because Kate's killer took it. Then it was on Tilly Franklin's arm. So, you're telling me you didn't arrest her?"

My heart is racing. Why is he discounting this valuable piece of information?

Jack crosses his arms and shakes his head. "I've already said too much. The bottom line is you have to stay out of this, Maddie."

"Jack, Kate was Jenna's friend. Her killer has robbed my mother of her home and the businesses of our event venue. You can't expect me not to do all I can to discover who did this. This is personal, Jack."

"Yeah, it'll get real personal when you cause me to lose my job."

My mouth falls open. "Are you saying because we're engaged, I have to passively sit by while you ignore evidence like that custom-made bracelet on Tilly Franklin's arm? Kate was wearing that bracelet the night she died. Someone took it off of a dead woman's arm. The only person who would've had access to it was Kate's killer."

"Yet, she didn't appear the least bit nervous wearing it around two police officers," Jack counters.

"Of course not," I say. "That would've tipped her hand. You surprised her. It's not as if she dresses for your meeting. She had no choice but to act like it was nothing. Think about it, Jack."

He sighs. It's the most exasperated sound I've ever heard from him. He leans forward, braces his elbows on his knees, puts his head in his hands, and rubs his eyes.

"It's been a long day, Maddie. I can't do this right now. I came over to spend some time with you. The last thing I want to do is argue."

"You say you came over to spend time with me, but the first thing you did was reprimand me." I know that is the wrong thing to say the minute the words left my mouth, so I decide to go for broke. "Until we got engaged, you never had a problem talking to me about investigations. It helps me with the books I write. And on the occasion that the crimes have touched my life, I have worked to help you solve them. I've always handed all the evidence over to you. I've never tried to apprehend the perp or take credit for solving the cases. But you must admit that several times I've handed you pieces of the puzzle you didn't see—"

He stands up. "I have to go."

"So, you're just going to leave?" I ask. "You don't even want to talk about this?"

He closes his eyes and opens them slowly as if he's calling on every ounce of patience he possesses. "Not right now," he finally says.

"Please, Jack, let's talk about this."

He hesitates but sits down.

"I understand where you're coming from," I say. "I know you're stressed and working as hard as you can, but I don't appreciate you giving me orders."

He stares at me for a few beats. His face is impassive. "Why would you endanger yourself and your daughter?"

"I'm always careful, Jack."

"Yeah, well, sometimes careful isn't good enough. That's why—" He snaps his mouth shut.

He doesn't have to say it. If he'd finished the sentence, I know he would've said, *That's why Carla is dead.*

Suddenly, things make sense.

"Jack, Carla died in the line of duty. Now that we're engaged, are you reacting this way because you fear the same thing will happen to me?"

His eyes flash. For a moment, I fear he'll get up and walk out.

Instead, a heart-wrenching look of sadness washes over

his handsome face.

"Yeah. I didn't realize it until now, but … yes."

This is a huge, heartbreaking breakthrough for us.

He's opening up to me, but I don't see how we can be happy if we want such different things.

"I started writing after Frank went missing," I say. "It was a way that I felt like I could control my world when so much was spinning out of control. In my books, I could right wrongs and bring killers to justice. It didn't change anything, but it was an escape when my world was crumbling around me."

He's watching me and listening in earnest.

"Over the years, I've learned that true crime is great fodder for my stories. Taking that one step further, I've gotten great satisfaction from personally investigating the handful of cases that have affected my life or the community that has always been there for me. Sleuthing has become a thread of the fabric that makes me who I am. I don't think I can change." Tears scald my throat because I realize there's no other way to say it. "I love you, Jack, but I can't promise you that I can be the woman you need."

"I know I've had trouble opening up to you." The anguish in his eyes is almost unbearable. "Since I lost Carla, I've become an island, handling everything myself."

"I guess we both have issues, huh?" I say.

He nods.

"I don't want to lose you, Jack, but I don't think either

of us is ready to get married again."

He starts to say something, but I hold up my hand.

"I'm not saying we'll never get there, but just not right now." My heart aches as I slide the ring off my finger and hold it out to him.

"Please don't give it back, Maddie. You don't have to wear it, but maybe you can put it on when you're ready to try again."

"How do I know *you'll* be ready?" I ask.

Before he can answer, I say, "Jack, I want you to keep the ring, and when we're both ready, you can propose again and…" I hold out the ring again.

My heart breaks a little more when he takes it.

"I know I have some issues to work on," he says.

"I do, too. In the meantime, let's consider our relationship a work in progress."

Chapter Eleven

~ *Jenna* ~

IAN IS BACK from California. He texted me today and asked me to have dinner with him. He'd made a reservation at Chez Paris, the fanciest restaurant in Hemlock.

Mom has been so sad over Jack that I felt terrible abandoning her to go on a date, but she insisted. Plus, Gigi is there. So, she's not entirely alone.

Ian and I haven't had much time together since London's wedding week and his trip out of town. Since he'd made a reservation at the nicest restaurant in Hemlock, I guess he's missed me as much as I've missed him.

When I ask him if we're celebrating something, he says, "That remains to be seen."

That remains to be seen.

What does that even mean?

Full disclosure. The possibility that he might propose stumbled through my head, but I sent it packing.

We are so not there yet.

Or are we?

The pros?

We're closer than ever. Ian moved to Hemlock so we could see each other more. He bought a house in Hemlock and, on several occasions, joked that I should move in with him—*umm*, thanks, but no.

He even kept his residence in Hemlock after the Asheville-based firm he works for offered him a junior partnership with the promise of becoming a full partner within five years.

The cons?

We've never said I love you.

But some people aren't comfortable saying the words. They show them.

Isn't walking the walk better than talking the talk?

So, as I sit across from him at the cozy table in Chez Paris in the best little black dress I own, red lipstick and my fingernails painted a matching shade complements of the coat of quick-dry polish I slapped on while I waited for him to pick me up—why is the proposal possibility still flirting with my imagination and making my stomach all fluttery?

Maybe it's because he just ordered a bottle of champagne. And he keeps glancing at me, looking nervous … but there's a certain gleam in his green eyes that I've never seen before.

Oh my gosh! Can this be happening?

At least three times, I start to ask him what's up, but the words get stuck in my throat.

After I think about it for a minute, it's a good thing I

didn't blurt out, *What's up?* Well, I wouldn't say it that way, though no matter how I put it, it might come across indelicately. Especially if he has something special planned.

Does he have something special planned?

Have I been *this* blind lately?

It might actually make sense. He made junior partner. Getting married would give him an air of responsibility—that he was settled in his life.

But do I love him enough to … to marry him?

I think I do.

I do.

The butterflies do another loop-de-loop through my stomach, causing me to inhale sharply.

"Are you okay?" he asks me.

"I am doing great," I say. "This is a pleasant surprise. And you look awfully handsome."

He does. Dressed in his gray suit with a white shirt and blue tie. I've always loved his smile. It might sound corny, but it really does light up a room.

"Thanks, and you look—" He blows a low whistle. "I'm the luckiest guy in the room."

The server delivers the champagne and takes our orders—Ian orders the boeuf bourguignon, and I choose one of the specials: shrimp and scallops in lobster sauce.

When the server leaves us alone, Ian holds my hand across the table. "I care about you, Jenna."

I hope he can't see the gooseflesh breaking out on my

arms.

"I'm so glad you're in my life," he continues.

I can't even respond because it's hard to breathe and my heart is thudding in my chest, dancing to a song that goes, *It's happening. This is it. It's happening. This is it.*

"That's why I hope we can try and make it work when I move to Los Angeles."

Wait. What?

His mouth is moving, and he's saying something about how he accepted a position with Evans and Reid, the LA law firm representing London. They were impressed with how he rose to the occasion with London's case and offered him a position.

"I understand if you don't want to do the long-distance thing," he says. "But I'd love it if we could give it a try. I'm not leaving for a month. I owe it to Stanley, Howard, and Cash to tie up all my loose ends."

Tie up loose ends.

Is that what I am? A loose end?

The voice of reason tries to remind me that he asked if we could continue our relationship long distance. Still, the reality that he made this decision—he signed on the dotted line so fast—and without even asking how I felt about it—levels a hard blow.

Here I am ready to say yes to a proposal.

Clearly, we are not on the same page in this relationship.

All I can say is, "You're leaving."

"Yes, but not for a month. I know we're both busy with our careers, but I hope we can carve out some time to spend together."

Tears burn the back of my throat, but I swallow them. Since he didn't include me in the decision, tears would be so inappropriate right now. I—I don't know what to do.

So, the only thing I can do is go on autopilot and stick to the perfunctory questions.

"What about your house? Will you sell it?"

He shrugs. "I'll give life in LA six months to see how it goes. During that time, I might try to rent out the house. But I'll need a place to stay when I come back to visit. And you'll visit, right? There's so much to see and do there. I've always thought of Los Angeles as the place where dreams come true. You can get anything you want in that city."

Yeah, as opposed to Hemlock, where you just get me.

Stop it! You will not let him see you feeling sorry for yourself.

When Ian drops me off, I don't invite him in.

I could have since I'm back in the lower half of the house, and Gigi is staying upstairs with Mom.

Instead, I feigned exhaustion and told him I needed to catch up on work, which I suppose is true, even if the two excuses don't support each other.

The funny thing is, he didn't try to change my mind.

He's always been good at reading people, and I'm sure he could sense that my *I'm happy if you're happy* wasn't exactly a resounding celebration of his news.

I go inside and get ready for bed, but I lie there tossing and turning.

Finally, I venture upstairs.

I hear Mom and Gigi chatting in the living room.

"Now that I'm back in town permanently, I'd love to rejoin the Hemlock Ladies' League," she says. "I pulled an application offline, but it says I need two sponsors who are members in good standing and are not related to me."

"I'm sure Val will be happy to sponsor you."

Valorie Anderson is Mom's best friend. She also happens to be my godmother and Ian's aunt. While she's not related to us by blood, she might as well be because she's like family. Val is the family we chose.

"Knock-knock," I say. "I'm sure Tess would sponsor you, too."

"Look who's home," Gigi says. "Did you have a nice night with your beau?"

"It was fine." I force my lips into a smile.

When Mom and Gigi stare at me, I say, "It was great. A real treat."

"Well, good," Gigi says.

She's still looking at me like I'm not telling the truth. Of course, I'm not, but since Mom's having trouble with Jack, I don't want to whine about my boyfriend moving and asking for a long-distance relationship.

The sharp jab of how he didn't even ask me how I felt about the move before he accepted the position needles my heart again. I know I should look at the positive, but I think it's best to change the subject right now.

"I'm glad you want to rejoin the league, Gigi. I'm sure they'll welcome you with open arms. You can go with us to the meeting next week. Between now and then, Mom and I will ask Val and Tess about sponsoring you. Don't be surprised if they hit you up to hold the annual gala at Gracewood Hall."

"There's a thought," Gigi says. "It might sweeten the pot when it comes down to whether or not they'll readmit me."

"Venue or no venue, I'm sure they'd love to have you back," Mom says.

"Even if it's a murder scene before it officially opens?" Gigi asks. "I remember how some of the ladies ganged up on Jenna after that ex-boyfriend of hers died."

"I'd like to think they learned their lesson," I say. "Plus, you aren't a suspect in Kate's murder. I was … for about thirty seconds, when Riley Buxston died."

It's true. One moment, the town rallied around me because they were sure I was mourning the loss of my best chance to marry well. Never mind that Riley and I hadn't dated since we were eighteen. When he was found dead the morning of his wedding, half the town was sure I did it in a fit of jealousy.

I didn't, of course.

"Well, only a ninny could suspect you of murder," Gigi says.

"Speaking of murder, I have an interesting update," Mom says. "Jack came by tonight and said they did not arrest Tilly Franklin because Tilly said David gave her the bracelet."

"Well, according to David, Tilly is not very balanced," I say. "Of course, she would say something like that. We need to call David and let him know what she said. But wait a minute. Jack came by?"

I study her as she nods. Her poker face is firmly in place. She's not giving away anything.

"I have so many questions," I say. "I don't even know which one to ask first."

"I'll make it easy on you," Mom says, and she tells me about what transpired with Jack.

"Oh, no," I say.

You gave back the ring?

He took it?

Does that mean it's over?

It can't be over.

You two are too good together.

I hurt for her, and my thoughts are stuck in my head. I'm afraid that anything I say will make it worse. Now that I know what's happened, I can see that her calm is a fragile façade that could break under the weight of the wrong words.

"He's attracted to badass women."

Mom's smile is melancholy. "I am a badass, aren't I? But

Jack doesn't want me to be one."

She swallows hard.

"I'm sorry," I say as a tear breaks free and meanders down my cheek. I swipe it away. "If misery loves company, Ian took me to dinner tonight to tell me he's moving to Los Angeles."

Mom and Gigi gasp.

I tell them what transpired, and while it's not a breakup, we aren't the power couple I thought we were since he didn't even ask me how I felt about the move.

Sweet Gigi says, "Oh, dear. I'm sorry, lovey." She pulls me into a hug. When she lets loose, she says, "I hate it when my girls are sad. I know you two are close, but it's rather uncanny that you would coordinate your man trouble schedule. I think this calls for something drastic. While you were in Asheville today, I replenished our stash of Ben & Jerry's. Maybe I was having a premonition? Cherry Garcia, anyone?"

Geeg doesn't even bother with bowls. She comes back with three pints and three spoons and distributes them.

"I have news myself," Gigi says. "I told your mother earlier, but that nice detective Jeff Salisbury called me and said that Gracewood Hall was no longer a crime scene. We're free to return."

Her words hang in the air.

"Do you want to go back?" I ask. "I mean, to live?"

"I'm not sure how you feel, dear," Gigi says. "As much as

I love Gracewood Hall, I don't relish the thought of living there right now. Not so soon after the murder. Your lovely mother has offered to let me stay here for a while. I've taken an oath that I will not get in her hair. Will you move back home, too?"

"Of course," I say. "It's nice that we can be together."

"It is nice," Mom says.

I can see the sadness in her eyes.

"Why don't we do something tomorrow," I suggest. "Let's pamper ourselves and stuff ourselves with our favorite comfort food. What do you say?"

"Or we could take a trip to Greenville, South Carolina, and pay a visit to Greg Paulson, and show Ian you might just be too busy to miss him."

~ Jenna ~

LAST NIGHT, I texted David to see if he had any updates.

He didn't answer. Granted, it was late. He was probably asleep.

I'd wanted to tell him we were going to Greenville to talk to Greg Paulson this morning, but something kept me from putting it in writing. I don't know him that well.

While I'm confident he didn't kill Kate—he has a solid alibi—I never put anything in writing that I wouldn't mind sharing with all humankind. Or, in this case, Jack. If he knew we were going to see Paulson, it would only make matters worse between him and Mom. I'm holding out for them to get back together.

However, I do trust Tess implicitly. On the drive to Greenville, I text her about our newly hatched plan. I give her Greg Paulson's address and tell her that I'll check in with her when we arrive and let her know as soon as we're finished.

Before we left, I called Greg Paulson's office to see if I could schedule an appointment.

At first, the receptionist told me that Mr. Paulson was out of the office today but could see me first thing tomorrow morning. With a bit of persistence and insistence that I was only available today, she relented and worked me into the schedule for the early afternoon.

"If Greg Paulson is in South Carolina today, that means he's not following David around Raleigh," I say. "I wonder if Tilly called off the dogs now that Kate is no longer a threat."

"Would it be weird for Tilly to know Kate is..." Mom trails off and clears her throat. It's still as difficult for her to say it as it is for me. "It's only been a few days."

"Yeah, but news like this travels fast," I say. "Think of all the people who were at the rehearsal dinner the night Kate died, and there was the crowd that was hanging out outside the gates of Gracewood Hall the next morning."

"True, but we never discerned whether those were people who were invited to the wedding since London had agreed to send out a text blast to the guests telling them the wedding was off."

"But London was talking about it on social media," I say. "Thank goodness she didn't give too much identifying information about Kate, but people still talk, and word gets around."

We're silent for a moment as we're both processing this.

"But wait," I say. "As far as I know, Jack still hasn't released Kate's name to the press, and Kate wasn't contracted to be in London's wedding until Thursday. Even in London's melodramatic video, she didn't mention Kate's last name. How would Tilly have gotten word that Kate was dead? Unless somehow Greg Paulson knew and told her."

"And unless Greg Paulson has an inside source, how would he know? Unless he did it."

Mom slants a quick glance at me.

"Or Tilly killed Kate," I offer.

"Either way, we need to be very careful because we don't know what we're dealing with here," Mom says.

"It just hit me," I say. "What if he recognizes you from when he caught you snooping around his car at the Hemlock Inn? I think it might be smart if I went in alone."

"Not on your life," Mom says. "We still haven't ruled out that he's the killer. Even if Tilly was the one who did it, we don't know what their relationship is. They could be in on it together. We are doing this together, or we're not doing it at all."

After we arrive in Greenville, we use the time before our appointment to discuss the merits of being straightforward with Paulson about why we're meeting with him rather than making up a story about why we need to hire a PI.

We decide to split the difference and tell Greg we'd like to hire him to follow my ex-boyfriend, David Martin. We figure his initial reaction to another of David's exes hiring him might offer some kind of tell. Also, we agree that if push comes to shove, we will come clean and tell him that we were looking into the murder of Kate Asher and ask for his help.

My heart is pounding as we park in front of Greg Paulson's office, which is located in a corner unit of a rundown strip shopping center. If you weren't looking for the place, you might not even realize it's a private investigator's office. Unlike the other storefront shops, Paulson's unit is located around the corner of the building. Fronted by one window shrouded by what looks like blackout curtains, the office has a plain, solid front door marked by a unit number. There isn't a sign, and we have to press an intercom buzzer for assistance.

"I'm glad we called for an appointment," Mom says. "That was good thinking. Otherwise, we might not have gotten inside."

A female voice answers the intercom. "May I help you?"

I stifle a nervous laugh. I feel like she might ask us for a password like they used to use in the days of speakeasies.

"Hello, I'm Jenna Bell. I have an appointment with Mr.

Paulson."

A buzzer and a click sound by way of an answer. I pull the door open, and Mom and I step inside a dank office, which smells of mildew, burnt coffee, and stale cigarette smoke.

When my eyes adjust to the dim light, I see a brunette with chin-length hair raised at the crown in a way reminiscent of those bumpit hair volumizing tools that were popular in the mid-2000s. She's wearing red thick-frame glasses and matching lipstick. The old-fashioned metal desk where she's stationed adds to her retro look. The entire tableau makes it difficult to assess her age, which could be anywhere from thirty-five to fifty. I get the eerie feeling that we've stepped back in time.

She holds up a clipboard. "Fill out these papers. Mr. Paulson will see you in a moment. You can sit over there."

She gestures to a row of four chairs lining the wall to the left of the front door.

We have seated ourselves when she asks, "How will you pay today?"

I look up from the clipboard and blink at her, but she's looking down, writing something in a journal.

"What's the fee?" I ask.

"It's fifty bucks for the initial consultation, and if Mr. Paulson takes your case, it's one hundred bucks an hour," she says without looking up from the ledger in which she's writing. The scene hits me as old school as the old desk and her retro glasses. "Cash or charge? There's a three percent fee for the convenience of using a credit card."

Wow. Super convenient for them.

"Oh, okay," I say. "I just realized I don't know your name."

She looks up. "It's Brenda. Cash or charge?" she repeats.

"I wish you had mentioned the consultation fee when we spoke on the phone earlier; I would've picked up some cash."

She doesn't answer me.

I open my purse to take out my credit card, but Mom says, "I have cash." She stands up to give it to Brenda, who puts it in the top middle desk drawer.

"May I have a receipt, please?" Mom asks.

"Oh." Brenda gazes at her as if she's asked her to make her a banana split.

Before Brenda can comply, a door across from where I'm sitting opens.

"Jenna Bell?" a stocky bald man with a gray handlebar mustache calls from the doorway. He's wearing jeans and sunglasses on top of his head. His twin tattoo sleeves are visible from where the edge of his black T-shirt clings to his beefy biceps.

I suddenly have the urge to leave rather than enter his office, which now feels like a lion's den, but Mom is intrepidly walking toward him, and I have no choice but to follow because I'm not letting her go in there alone.

I'm glad she was so insistent about us doing this together.

As I approach him, he gestures to the clipboard I'm carrying.

"I didn't have a chance to complete the form," I say.

He grunts and takes it anyway and then nods to the chairs in front of his desk. "What's up, ladies?" he asks. "Brenda said you're only in town today, and you urgently needed to see me. What's the story?"

He has such a poker face that I can't tell whether or not he recognizes Mom from the night he caught her snooping around his car. Even if he does remember her, would he tip his hand?

"I want to hire you to follow my ex-boyfriend," I say in a rush of words.

"Ex-boyfriend?" he asks. "If he's an ex, why do you need me to tail him?"

We really should've thought this through better because I don't know what to say.

"He took something from my daughter," Mom fills in.

With the same expressionless demeanor, Paulson asks, "If he stole from you, maybe it's a matter for the police."

"No, I don't want to get the police involved," I say.

Paulson picks up a pen. "Where does he live?"

"Asheville," I say.

"Asheville," he repeats. "Why do you want to hire me? I charge for mileage and time on the road. Out-of-town surveillance can add up. If you want me to rough him up or break in, I don't do anything illegal. I'm still not sure what you're expecting."

"Okay, so it's not really a thing he took from me. Not an object, anyway. It's more like my dignity. He humiliated me. He was cheating on me with a woman named Kate Asher, and I want to know if they're still together."

Paulson stares at me for an interminable moment. My heart pounds so hard, I'm afraid he can see it dancing beneath my pink cotton blouse. What if he remembers me from the morning he buzzed through Gracewood Hall? Even though Kate beelined inside, I was standing outside near the driveway when he drove by.

I wish I could backpaddle and not say Kate's last name. I hold my breath, trying to calm down, but the horse is out of the barn now. There's no taking it back.

He narrows his eyes. "Kate Asher, huh?"

I nod.

He looks at the paper, which only has my name on it. After paying Brenda, that was as far as I got filling in the information.

"What's this ex-boyfriend's name?"

I clear my throat. "David Martin."

It's not a unique name. There are probably thousands of David Martins in the world and maybe dozens in the Asheville area.

"David Martin from Asheville," he says.

I nod.

"David Martin from Asheville cheated on you with Kate Asher?"

I nod again, holding my breath as I wait for him to admit he's heard the names before, or that another of his clients has had issues with a David Martin from Asheville. But it would be unprofessional of him to talk about another client. It would probably violate client confidentiality laws.

Are private detectives bound by such laws?

"I'll need some information about these two," he says. "Like their home addresses and a general idea of where they go in a week. If you know where they meetup it would be helpful."

"So, you'll take my case?"

"Yeah, why not?" He shrugs. "If you've got the money. I've gotta make bank."

"And what will I get for … this money… that I'm spending … for you to trail David Martin … my ex-boyfriend?"

It's barely perceptible, but I'm sure I see him wrinkle his nose for a fraction of a second. Then, just as quickly, his gaze flits to my mom and back to me.

"You'll get photographs of them together. I can't promise anything salacious, but I'll grab a shot if I see them together. If I don't see them together, you won't get anything, but I still get paid. Speaking of, I'll need a retainer up front."

He scribbles something on a sheet of paper and slides it across the desk.

My eyes probably bug out of my head like a cartoon character when I look at the unbelievable amount. I realize too late that he's called my bluff.

"You wanna cut to the chase and tell me why you're really here, ladies?"

When I don't speak, he asks, "London Brinks wouldn't happen to be a friend of yours, would she?"

"How do you know London?" Mom asks.

Paulson clicks the pen he used to write down the exorbitant sum earlier. "Isn't it her life's mission for everyone to know her? Look, the police have already been here. I told them everything I know. Why are you here?"

I raise my chin and look him in the eyes. "Kate was my friend. It seems like the police aren't doing enough."

Click-click. Click-click. Click-click. Click-click.

"So, y'all are in the investigative business looking into your friend's death?" he asks.

"You might say that." I sound much braver than I feel.

Click-click. Click-click. Click-click. Click-click.

"Yeah, I also might say that you're poking your nose into murder. Most murderers don't like it when someone does that. If they've killed once, they don't have much to lose by killing again."

Click-click. Click-click. Click-click. Click-click.

Goose bumps break out all over my body. Is this guy Kate's killer? Maybe he and Tilly are in it together.

He tosses the pen onto the desk with a flick of his wrist.

"Look, I'm just sayin' this isn't a good hobby for a couple of nice ladies like you and your friend London. That *Who Killed Kate* stunt of hers has gone viral. Even the press is picking it up. You might want to tell her she'd better watch herself."

"Are you threatening her?" Mom asks.

"On the contrary, I am warning her."

Chapter Twelve
~ Maddie ~

KATE'S MEMORIAL SERVICE happens on Friday in Asheville, exactly one week after she was killed.

It's lovely and heartfelt, even though Kate isn't actually there. The coroner hasn't yet released her body.

"It's sort of fitting that we're here and Kate is somewhere else," Ruth says in a shaky voice to the small group that's gathered in a bricked area of a rose garden in Jefferson Park in Asheville to celebrate Kate's life.

Ruth is a fine-boned blonde. I can see the resemblance to her sister, but Ruth is slighter than Kate. Where Kate's confidence seemed to fill a room, Ruth appears to be folding in on herself, as if trying to make her petite body even smaller.

Of course, her posture could be due to the fact that she's memorializing her sister.

Among about three dozen people who have turned out today, Anson and London, who is wearing a wide-brimmed black straw hat tied with a white silk scarf and sunglasses like she's Audrey Hepburn in *Breakfast at Tiffany's*, are sitting in the front row. David is sitting in the back row of the folding chairs that have been set up.

"Kate always seemed to have bigger and better places to go and things to do in life," Ruth continues. "After college, we took different paths in life. I was settled with my family. Kate was determined to conquer the business world. Of course, she had recently reunited with someone special."

Ruth gestures to David. Everyone turns and looks at him. He's sitting by himself, hunched over with his forearms braced on his knees. His head is down.

"David, would you like to say a few words about Kate?"

It seems like an olive branch. A nice gesture.

He glances up, and I can see that he's crying. He waves off the offer and ducks his head again.

"Oh, of course," Ruth murmurs. "I'm so sorry, David. I know losing Kate has been hard on you, too."

The empathy in her voice sounds sincere.

I didn't expect Ruth Asher Long to stand up and defame her sister, but this woman, who had said that Kate had it coming, didn't appear to be the shrew that David had made her out to be. Then again, sometimes people wear masks in public.

Or they react badly out of shock.

"I regret that my sister and I weren't closer," she says. "There was the geographical distance, of course. I'm in Savannah and Kate's here—umm—was here. In Asheville. I have kids and she was determined to conquer the business world. But I've already said that. Since I'm starting to repeat myself, I'll close with this. Tomorrow is not guaranteed. If you have a beef with someone who means something to you, don't wait to make up. Because you may not get the chance." A sob catches the last word, and she takes a moment to compose herself. "There are some light refreshments in the back," she says. "I hope you'll stay and tell me how you knew my sister and share your memories of her."

A singer begins the first strains of an acapella "Amazing Grace." Ruth and a man, who I'm guessing is her husband, usher two little girls to the back of the open-air chapel. People begin to stand and approach the Long family to offer condolences. I look to see if David is standing with them, but he's not there.

Jenna and I hang back to be the last to talk to Ruth. I am curious to know if Jack has interviewed her or if she has an alibi. Of course, I have no intentions of launching into an interrogation here, but I'm hoping she won't mind if I ask her a few questions.

"Ruth, I'm so sorry for your loss," I say. "I'm Maddie Bell, and this is my daughter, Jenna Bell."

Ruth's mouth forms a perfect oh. "You called the house a couple of times this week. I'm so sorry I didn't return your call. As you can imagine, I've been a bit preoccupied with the memorial arrangements and gathering my sister's belongings. It has been difficult on so many levels. I hope you understand." She swallows hard.

"Of course," I say.

"Ruth, I went to college with Kate," Jenna offers.

"Oh, then you might know Kate's college roommate, Polly."

Kate calls to Polly, who joins us.

"Can I get you something, Ruth?" Polly asks.

"No, thank you. Baxter has gone to get me a glass of wine. This is Jenna Bell. She knew Kate in college, and I thought you two might know each other."

Polly squints at Jenna and shakes her head. "I don't think so. But it's been a few years. Have we met?"

"No. Kate and I had several classes together, and we often collaborated on projects since we were both interested in the wedding industry, but we didn't hang out that much outside of class."

Ruth smiles, but the sadness is apparent in her eyes. "Where are you two from?"

"We're from Hemlock, North Carolina," Jenna says. "It's about forty-five minutes south of Asheville."

Ruth's jaw drops. "Was it your wedding in which she was acting as maid of honor?"

"Well, it was a wedding that I was facilitating," Jenna answers.

"It was my wedding," London says. "I'm sorry to interrupt, but I need to scoot. I flew in from my honeymoon to honor Kate, and we're going back. Our flight leaves at six. I wanted to say how heartbroken I am for you—for your loss. Kate was a new friend, and I'm so sorry I didn't get to know her better."

Jenna and I exchange a knowing glance. I'm still wondering why she cut her Cabo vacay short to attend a memorial service for a woman she'd known less than twenty-four hours.

Something smells funny.

"I'm so upset over all that's happened," London says. "I don't know if you've seen my social media channels, but I'm offering a reward to anyone who gives the police information leading to the arrest of Kate's killer. In fact, I've decided I'm doubling the reward. I'll make the announcement later today, and I would be honored if you would stand with me when I do."

Ruth seems to shrink even more after hearing London's request. She tries to convince London that no means no, and I jump in and change the subject.

"Ruth, in addition to offering my condolences, one of the reasons I called you earlier in the week is that my daughter and I are conducting our own investigation into Kate's murder."

Ruth flinches.

Polly and London lean in.

"We're doing this with the purest intentions," Jenna says. "Kate was my friend, and I want to find out who did this. When was the last time you saw Kate?"

Ruth inhales and glances up and to the left. According to body language experts, this indicates she's trying to recall the answer. A glance up and to the right would signal a fabrication.

"Honestly, it's been so long ago. I can't really recall."

"More than a decade?" I ask.

She nods and hangs her head.

"Ruth, forgive me," Jenna says. "Where were you last Friday night?"

A man walks up and hands Ruth a glass of white wine. "She was at work all day, and then she was at home with me and our children. I'm her husband, Baxter Long, and you are?"

We introduce ourselves as Baxter glowers at us.

"Ladies, we've already given our statement to the police. My wife is already feeling fragile because of the loss. If you don't mind."

He smiles and turns his back on us, shielding Ruth with his body.

"I think this is a good time to get a drink," Jenna says.

"Uhh-huh," I say. "I would suggest we leave, but I'd like to talk to Polly."

At the drinks table, we each pour glasses of sparkling water and then retreat to a corner where we can observe.

"It takes about five hours to get to Hemlock from Savannah. That would be a ten-hour round trip. Not unheard of. The wrinkle is if she hadn't spoken to her sister in a decade, how would she know Kate would be in Hemlock? Don't forget how last minute it was that we booked her for the wedding. One day's notice, and she was supposed to have been in another wedding, but she said she switched with a colleague when I called."

"I didn't know that," I say.

Jenna grimaces. "I'd forgotten it until now."

"This case has so many moving pieces and parts, it's no wonder," I say. "By the way, where's David?"

Jenna glances around. "I have no idea. I haven't seen him since the service ended. Maybe he's too emotional right now. I still can't get over London flying all the way from Cabo to attend a memorial service of a woman she'd known for less than a day, and now she's flying back."

We exchange a look that says, *that's weird*.

"Jenna, Maddie." London teeters over in black patent leather Louboutin stilettos. Anson hangs back, as silent as ever. His attention is trained on his phone.

"Oh, this is so, so, so, so, sad," London says.

She pulls a tissue out of her quilted Chanel bag and dabs under the large frames of her sunglasses.

"It is sad," Jenna says. "But you came all the way from Cabo San Lucas to attend the funeral?"

"I did." She dabs at her eyes again. "I didn't know Kate very long, but her senseless death has affected me. It's changed me. Listen, loves, we're heading back to Cabo. I have to run, but talk soon."

She leans in and blows air kisses, somehow keeping her big black hat in place.

We watch her walk away on Anson's arm. She stops outside of the rose garden, takes out her phone, and holds it in front of her face. Even though I can't hear her, I can tell by her animated movements that she's livestreaming.

"At least she had the good grace not to broadcast the memorial service," I say. "I know she's been cleared, but I can't help but think there's something more to her that none of us is seeing. She's overplaying this role she's created for herself."

"A little too much, if you ask me," Jenna says. "It's beginning to border on *the lady doth protest too much, methinks*. Even though the lab cleared her and she's no longer a suspect, something feels off with her."

"I agree," I say. "There's Polly. Why don't we talk to her while she's alone?"

Polly is sitting in one of the folding chairs, balancing a small plate of cheese and fruit on her lap and holding a glass of white wine.

"How long did you and Kate room together in college?" Jenna asks.

"All four years. We started as dormmates freshman year, and then we moved to an apartment." She pops a grape into her mouth.

"You must've known her pretty well."

Polly nods.

"Did you two keep in touch after college?"

Polly shrugs as she swallows the bite. "Here and there. Social media helps. It makes you feel plugged into someone's life even when you're not. Though after Kate's business took off, she posted less and less. I guess it was a privacy thing. She had to be discreet due to the nature of her business."

We nod and make small talk about our jobs. Polly is a buyer for a large department store chain, which explains her impeccable style. Today, she opted for a navy sheath dress and navy slingback pumps with a white toe cap. Her shiny auburn hair hangs in a perfect chin-length bob. Her red lipstick gives her an effortlessly chic look.

"You must've known David Martin," I say. "He was here a moment ago. Did you get a chance to say hello?"

Polly's eyes darken. "I know David. I'm surprised he had the nerve to show up today after what he did to Kate."

After what he did to Kate? What did he do?

"How did he find out about the service?" Polly asks. "I'm sure Ruth didn't call him."

Chills snake up and down my spine. There's more story here than Polly is telling us, and I am determined not to let her get away until she tells us everything.

"Did you know that Kate and David were seeing each other again?" I ask.

Polly rears back like I slapped her. "No way."

Both Jenna and I nod. "She didn't tell you?"

"Are you kidding me? If she had, I would've tried to talk

some sense into her. That guy is a sociopath. He was not a good boyfriend. He was abusive. After they broke up, Kate had to start seeing a therapist on campus. It was not pretty. How did she end up getting mixed up with that guy again?"

All three of us glance around, looking for David, no doubt, but he's not there.

Since neither Ruth nor Polly seem to think much of him, that's probably why he chose not to stick around.

"I guess people can change," I say.

Polly shrugs and stands. "Yeah, but a leopard can't change his spots. Look, if you'll excuse me, I need to go. I'm catching a train back to New York tonight and need to start heading toward the station."

"We're happy to give you a lift," I say.

"I appreciate it, but I've already hired a car. It should be here soon."

"Polly, before you go," Jenna says. "I don't mean to be indelicate, but would you happen to remember the name of the therapist on campus that Kate saw?"

Polly's eyes widen. "Funny you should ask, I do remember. I double-majored in fashion design and English literature, so it sort of stuck with me. Her name was Elizabeth Bennett."

"Interesting," Jenna says. "I wondered if Mrs. Bennett was her therapist. Kate and I never talked about it, but when I was in college, I saw Elizabeth Bennett, too. My father was in the Navy, and his plane was shot down. He was missing for years. Elizabeth Bennett helped me a lot. That is a name that's hard to forget."

Maybe Elizabeth Bennett can give us some insight into this other side of the charming David Martin that we haven't seen.

~ *Jenna* ~

AS LUCK WOULD have it, Elizabeth Bennett still works at the university.

When I call her, she remembers me and is happy to make an appointment for me to visit.

She didn't ask, and I didn't mention exactly what I wanted to talk to her about. I figured it would be better to tell her in person because it would be harder for her to brush me off if I was sitting in her office.

The Wednesday after Kate's memorial service, Tess and I road trip it to Chapel Hill. It's about a four-hour drive, so it gives us a chance to catch up.

We have both been busy and I hadn't told her about Ian's plans to move to Los Angeles before now.

"Aww, honey, I'm so sorry. I know this is not what you wanted. But it doesn't mean it's over. Sometimes things like this can make a relationship."

"Or break it," I mutter.

"I know this isn't what you want to hear, but if you two

do break up, wouldn't it be better for that to happen sooner rather than later? There's nothing worse than spending the best years of your life with a guy only to find out the two of you were never on the same page to begin with."

"Do you think Ian and I are not on the same page?"

"I didn't say that because I have no idea if you are or aren't. You two seem good together, but you are the only one who can answer that question."

One of the many things I love about Tess is her plainspoken honesty. I always know where I stand with her. A girl needs a friend like that in her life.

She's right. Have I not been facing the facts? Maybe Ian and I have stalled because we are at the end of the line, and neither wants to hurt the other.

That doesn't feel entirely right. Maybe it is one of those things where I have to let him go to see if we are meant to be. Perhaps I'll end up being the one who moves on. Only time will tell.

It's funny, though. When you're with someone, you never really know if it will be the last time you see that person. We don't dwell on things like that because it would be morbid, but I do think about it sometimes.

I can't clearly remember the last time I saw my dad. I know he'd been home on leave before shipping out to Afghanistan, but I don't remember the last moments or last words we said to each other. I'd like to believe it was *I love you*. Or even *see you soon*, but if I had known that was the last time I would see him, I would've committed those final moments to memory like a movie I could take out at will and replay in my head when I needed him.

I shake off the maudlin cloud that's threatening to settle around me. For the rest of the four-hour trip, Tess and I keep the conversation light. We laugh and talk in a way that feels normal for the first time since Kate died and Ian dropped the LA bomb.

When we arrive at the university, I only have about fifteen minutes to spare before I meet with Mrs. Bennett.

"You go do your thing," Tess says. "I've always wanted to see the campus. Can you believe I've lived in North Carolina my whole life, and this is my first time here? Text me when you're finished, and we'll meet up."

Elizabeth Bennett is friendly, but professionally distant, as she welcomes me into her office. Various diplomas hang on the wall. If I remember correctly, they're in the same place that they were the last time I was in her office years ago.

The furniture is different, though.

"Please sit down, Jenna." She gestures to a chintz floral-covered sofa.

I sit down while she chooses a chair that complements the sofa. She looks relaxed as she peers at me through her frameless glasses.

I notice the silver streaks in her dark hair. They weren't there the last time we spoke. I hadn't thought about it before, but she's probably older than my mom but younger than Gigi. Besides her hair, which she still wears in a French twist, she is still the same warm, well-dressed woman I remember.

"It's lovely to see you."

We make small talk. I catch her up on what I'm doing these days and tell her about my father, and now that I know he did not survive the plane crash, I've been able to come to terms with the loss.

"Of course. I'm sure it was difficult living in limbo all those years."

I nod. "But that's not why I'm here today, Mrs. Bennet."

"Do call me Elizabeth, please. What brings you in today?"

What she doesn't say is *I haven't heard from you in nearly a decade. What do you want?*

"Do you remember a student named Kate Asher?" I ask. "She went to school here at the same time I did. She was a patient of yours."

Elizabeth's smile fades into a straight line. "I can't say I remember the name off the top of my head. I have seen a lot of clients over the years, but Jenna, before we go any further, I must tell you that I am not in the habit of discussing my clients—past or present."

"I thought you might say that." I steeple my hands in my lap. "Elizabeth, Kate was murdered last week."

I stand and hand her a copy of the obituary I clipped

from the *Asheville Citizen–Times* newspaper.

She studies it.

Her face softens. "Yes, I remember her face. But I see so many students I don't recall what we discussed."

"Kate was a friend, and she was murdered during a wedding I planned. At her memorial service, I spoke with her college roommate, who told me that a guy Kate had dated in college had been abusive, and that was one of the reasons she came to you for help. I was hoping that you could answer a few questions."

Elizabeth shifts, and I sense she is about to close down the meeting.

"How about this?" I say. "What if I tell you everything I know, and maybe you can tell me if it rings a bell."

Again, she shifts and starts to speak, but I beat her to the punch.

"Before you say no, I looked up the regulations on patient confidentiality after a patient is deceased. In North Carolina, I believe you wouldn't be violating any laws by helping me get to the bottom of this case."

"I'm sorry. Are you with law enforcement, or are you in the private investigation field?" she asks. "I thought you said you were an event planner."

"It is my business to help law enforcement get to the bottom of who killed my friend. Since you knew her, I thought—I'd hoped—that you would want to help bring Kate's killer to justice."

I tell her about David showing up at London's wedding, that he seems charming and completely contrary to the ugly picture Polly had painted, but he had disappeared after the memorial service.

"Technically, he has an alibi for the time of the murder," I say. "But what Kate's roommate told me added to a couple of potential discrepancies. It doesn't settle right with me. I need to know if David was as abusive as Kate's roommate made him sound. If that's the case, I can't see Kate getting back together with him. She was a strong woman and had everything going for her. But something doesn't add up."

Especially when we add in the large amount of cash the police found in her room, but I won't share that information with her.

Elizabeth stares at the photo and sighs. "It's so sad that such a promising young woman was cut down in her prime."

I don't answer. I let her words hang in the air.

Finally, she says, "Given the circumstances and the fact that the patient is deceased, I'll look back at my records and see if anything stands out. I'll let you know if I find something."

Chapter Thirteen
~ Maddie ~

"I HAVE NO idea if I will hear from Elizabeth Bennett again," Jenna says. "She said she'd call if she discovered anything of interest, but that may have been her way of politely brushing me off."

Since Jenna's former counselor hasn't delivered anything substantive, and we didn't get a chance to talk to Tilly for any length of time, we decided to go back to Asheville and visit her, with the hopes that she'll open up and tell us her side of the story.

Because right now, I don't know what or whom to believe.

David painted an ugly picture of Tilly, but according to Polly, David is a monster. With each new card we turn over, David looks more suspect and less like Prince Charming, who reunited with his beloved Kate.

Kate, who is dead.

On top of the new speculation, David hasn't returned Jenna's and my texts and calls since we saw him at Kate's memorial service.

This time, we park farther away from Tilly Franklin's house. It's doubtful that Jack will show up here today, but out of an abundance of caution, we drove Jenna's car instead of mine and parked down the street and around the corner. Rather than right in front of the house as we did last time.

"Let's give Elizabeth a few more days," I say as I unlatch my seat belt. "If you haven't heard from her by the first of the week, I'd follow up. If you still get nothing, it might be a good idea to pass the information along to Jeff."

Jenna's eyebrow raises, and I know she's thinking, Jeff, not Jack, but I don't want to talk about it.

"Come on, let's go," I say. Before she can question me, I open my door, jump out of the car, and head toward Tilly's house.

When I reach her front door, I knock, but no one answers. So, I knock again.

"Looks like she's not home," Jenna says.

"Maybe." I knock again. "She'll be back sometime. Should we wait?"

"Sure," Jenna says. "You wait here in case she answers. I'll have a look around."

A moment later, the front door opens, but it's not Tilly. It's Jenna.

"What are you doing?" I ask. "How did you get inside?"

"The back door was unlocked. I called out hello. But no one answered. It's not breaking in if I enter through an unlocked door. I'm not sure that entering is a crime."

"That's debatable. You might want to talk to Betsy about that." I look left and then right to see if any of the neighbors are out, but as far as I can tell, the area is deserted. Not even a car drives by. "Let's get inside before someone sees us."

I step inside and then shut and lock the door behind us.

Tilly's house is as lovely on the inside as on the outside. It smells like lemon oil furniture polish and old money.

A living room opens to the right of the entryway, and a large office is to the left.

Expensive-looking rugs sit atop dark, polished hardwood floors. An antique grandfather clock that adorns a wall in the living room ticks loudly in the quiet. My heart thuds in time to its rhythm.

"How do you want to do this?" Jenna whispers. "Should we stick together or split up to cover more ground?"

"Let's split up."

"Okay, I'll take upstairs," Jenna says. "You look around down here."

"Put your cell phone on vibrate," I say, "so I can text you if she comes home."

"Or if she's upstairs … like sleeping or showering," Jenna whispers.

We both fall silent and listen, but I don't hear anything except for the air conditioner clicking on and the *tick-tocking* of the grandfather clock, which seems to count down the seconds we have left to explore.

I don't even know what we're looking for, except for something—anything—that proves that Tilly killed Kate.

"Okay, let's get to this," I murmur. "We should try to be out of here in five minutes or so. We need to work fast."

Jenna holds up five fingers. "Five minutes."

I walk around downstairs, taking it in a counterclockwise order, starting with the living room. I open end table drawers, open the front panel of the grandfather clock, run my hand over the top ledge, look under the edges of the Persian rug, and look under each item in the coffee tablescape—check under the fresh flower arrangement, shake out the large art books, look under the candles—but I find nothing. In this room, there aren't many places to snoop—it's furnished with expensive pieces, but it's minimal and perfect as a house in *Southern Living* magazine.

Next, I move to the formal dining room and—

What in the world?

Boxes of save-the-date cards with Tilly and David's faces smile up from ivory stock. In the photo, they're sitting on the front porch steps of this house. Kate is in front of David. He's leaning forward with his arms around her. They look so happy. So … in love.

The wedding date is New Year's Eve.

This is strange on so many levels. David said Tilly was the one maniacally pushing the wedding. He said he wanted nothing to do with it. Yet here he is, smiling like the eager, happy groom. I study the photo. It looks recent, but it could've been taken at any time.

There are boxes and boxes of cards. She's already started stuffing and addressing some envelopes in a gorgeous flowing script.

I pick up one of the envelopes and study it.

Wow. Tilly has talents. If she isn't a murderer, she could hire herself out. I'd be a wealthy woman if I had a dollar for every bride asking me to recommend a good calligraphist.

Tilly Franklin is a wealthy woman. I wonder why she's doing this herself rather than hiring someone to do it for her. But the ink well and dip pen are on the table. If she had hired out the job, the person wouldn't come to her house to do it.

Maybe it's her hobby.

I shrug. Whatever the case, she won't miss one of these.

I pluck a card from the box of those waiting to be stuffed and addressed, fold it in half, and stick it in the pocket of my jeans to show Jenna.

There's an open wedding planner. I thumb through it. I see where she's lined through Kate's name in the space to list the maid of honor. There's another woman's name written below it.

I flip back to the to-do list in the front of the book. She's already checked off *secure the wedding venue*. She's written in St. Andrews Catholic church. Above that, she has checked off dates to meet with the priest of the church.

Did David and Tilly go together?

I know a thing or two about weddings, and if a couple wants to be married in the Catholic church, they don't get a wedding date until they go through marriage prep and pass muster with the priest.

Does that mean that David went to the church with Tilly?

Or is she even sicker and more dangerous than David realizes to carry the charade this far?

Even though it's curious and concerning, it's not proof that Tilly killed Kate. I only have a few minutes left, and I need to finish searching downstairs for something more concrete.

I snap a few photos of her planner, returning everything as I found it, and move on to the open-concept kitchen and informal family room.

The first thing I spy is the La Cornue range, which is apropos of nothing except that I covet that appliance. I sigh. Hers is Provence blue, exactly the color I would choose if I could afford such an extravagance.

A pang of envy momentarily overrides my urgency to search quickly and leave the house. I walk over to it, run my hands over its luxurious surface, and curl my fingers around the sleek brass handle that runs the length of the range.

A top-of-the-line model can cost up to six figures. This one is smaller.

And it's still too pricy for my pocketbook.

On the surface, Tilly Franklin seems to have everything.

Why would she risk losing it all over a man who claims he doesn't return her affections?

Or does he?

Either way, if she killed Kate, she will go to jail. Unless she believes her money puts her above the law.

I tamp down my appliance-lust and scan the rest of the tidy kitchen. A collection of shiny brass pots and pans hangs above the range. Below that, sticking out of the wall, is a pot filler faucet. There's a marble-topped island in the center of the room with waterfall edges. The surfaces of all the countertops are shiny and uncluttered, except for a bowl of lemons in the center of the island and a crystal vase full of fresh pink peonies on the counter to the right of the sink.

As I turn to go into the family room, a piece of paper tucked under the peonies catches my eye.

It's a typed letter signed in blue ink.

When I read it, I have to hold onto the cold edge of the counter to keep my knees from buckling.

DEAR DAVID AND FAMILY,

IF YOU'RE READING THIS, I'M DEAD.

I'M SORRY.

I KNOW IT WILL COME AS A SHOCK, BUT I'M TOO RIDDLED WITH GUILT OVER KILLING KATE ASHER TO GO ON. I KNOW DAVID WILL NEVER UNDERSTAND WHY I HAD TO DO IT.

I HOPE YOU WILL BELIEVE ME WHEN I SAY IT

WASN'T MY IDEA TO KILL HER. GREG PAULSON, THE PRIVATE INVESTIGATOR I'D HIRED, INSISTED I GO TO GRACEWOOD HALL WITH HIM TO CONFRONT KATE. SHE ATTACKED ME.

NOW, GREG IS THREATENING TO BLACKMAIL THE FAMILY. THAT'S WHY I MUST KILL GREG, TOO. FIRST GREG AND THEN MYSELF. IT'S UNPLEASANT, BUT I HAVE NO OTHER CHOICE.

YOURS TRULY,
TILLY

My mind is whirling, and my hands shake as I text Jenna to come quickly.

Is Tilly's dead body upstairs?

Maybe Jenna hasn't gotten to that room yet.

I don't want her to stumble upon it alone. I should go up there rather than having her come downstairs only to go back up.

As I text, I turn around to go upstairs and collide with her.

I can't stifle my scream.

"It's okay. It's just me." Her words are barely a whisper. She's already moved through the kitchen and has one hand on the door. "Is someone home?" she whispers.

I shake my head and hold out the note with a trembling hand.

She crosses the floor and takes it. Her eyes grow large as

she reads.

"Tilly is dead? She admits to killing Kate and Greg?"

"Is her body upstairs?" I ask.

Jenna shakes her head emphatically. "I went into every room upstairs, and there is not a dead body."

"We need to call Greg and warn him," I say.

"I've got Greg's office number in my call history," Jenna says. "I'll call him, and you call the Greenville police and let them know."

Since we're in Asheville, calling 911 isn't the most expedient way to connect to Greenville's emergency services. Before I can look up the number, Jenna says, "Oh, no! I got his office voice mail."

As she leaves a frantic message for Greg, I find the number I need and call the Greenville emergency operator about the situation.

She takes my name and phone number.

After I hang up, I ask, "What do we do now?"

Jenna shrugs. "I don't know, but there was something weird upstairs."

I flinch.

She touches my arm. "No, not a dead body or anything like that. There's men's clothing in the primary bedroom closet and a bottle of *Acqua Di Parma* in the bathroom."

"That's the cologne David wears," I say. "You asked him about it when we had lunch last week. And look—Tilly's note was addressed to David and his family. Does he live here with her?"

Jenna shrugs. "Sort of looks that way."

If he doesn't, I wonder what his clone thinks of the save-the-date cards on the dining room table.

I start to tell her what I found in the dining room, but she says, "If Tilly killed herself and she's not here, where is she?"

"Maybe she went to a hotel or somewhere else?"

"Wait. Have you looked in the garage?" Jenna says.

I grimace. "No." The word comes out like a whimper. Because if Tilly Franklin has blown her brains out, I don't want to see it. I also don't want to have to call the police and explain what we're doing in her house.

Before I can gather my nerves, my brave daughter sets the suicide note on the counter and has already opened the door of the kitchen.

"No car in the garage. No body either."

I heave a whole-body sigh.

"You're sure you looked in every room?" I ask.

"Yes. This place is like a model home. It didn't take long to look in all the closets, under the beds, and behind the shower doors. I didn't see anything out of the ordinary except for the men's clothes and cologne.

"If Tilly did kill Kate, she probably got rid of the bottle that cracked her skull. I can't see her bringing it home. We saw the bracelet on her arm, but what else are we looking for? Unless she keeps a confessional diary."

Jenna rolls her eyes at the absurdity.

"I still haven't checked the office," I say.

"Let's have a look in there, and then let's get out of here," Jenna says. "We've been here a lot longer than five minutes. And I wonder if the Asheville police might show up here since you gave them Tilly's name and address."

"You're right. Let's get out of here."

I snap a shot of the note and tuck it under the vase of flowers, leaving it as I found it.

As we start toward the door, I'm stopped by a thought. "Wait a second, don't you find it weird that someone would type a suicide note?"

"I don't know. Is it weird?"

"It strikes me as strange. Think about it. If you were an emotional mess, would you sit at the computer and type out your goodbye, or would you do it longhand?"

"I've never thought about it."

The gorgeous display of calligraphy in the dining room crosses my mind. If that's Tilly's work, she would have a penchant for the pen.

I choose not to bring that up now because I want to find the computer she used to write the letter and see if it holds any answers. Then we need to get out of here.

The office walls are lined with beautiful built-in bookshelves, but the centerpiece is an opulent antique desk. With its inlaid wood, brass accents, and cabriole legs, it looks French—maybe Louie XV. It stands in front of a set of

French doors that lead outside. In the middle of the desk is a closed laptop.

"Bingo," I say under my breath as I approach the desk. "Now, if you will let us in without a password so I can have a nose around, that would be fabulous."

I pull out the medallion chair and take a seat. The desk is clean, except for the computer, a lamp, and a photo of Tilly and David—the same one that was on the save-the-date card.

I lift the computer's screen, and it hits me that we're leaving fingerprints all over Tilly's house, but it's too late now. When Jenna and I set out this morning, I had no idea that Tilly wouldn't be home, and we would have to sneak in to look for answers to our questions rather than simply asking her.

Now, there would be no asking her anything.

The computer chugs to life and immediately prompts me to enter a password.

"Darn. Not helpful." I glance around the room. "If you were Tilly Franklin, where would you store your passwords?"

"Check the desk drawers," Jenna suggests. "I've been checking the bookshelves, and I've got nothing here. There's not enough time to open every single book. I'm going for the wide sweep."

Even so, she continues to pull books off the shelf and flip through them.

I open the slim drawer in the center of the desk. An organizer holds neatly arranged office supplies. Underneath a small black leather notebook is a box of Crane's Crest stationery and an expensive fountain pen with spare ink cartridges. Additional proof that Tilly is a long-hander.

Why would a person capable of beautiful writing type out her last missive?

"I was going to tell you this later, but since the bookshelf is not giving us anything, go down the hall and look at what's on the dining room table."

Jenna's eyes widen.

"Don't worry, it's not a dead body, but another interesting piece to the puzzle."

"Okay. I'll be right back."

After she leaves, I pick up the little black book and murmur, "Please give me what I need."

As if my prayers are answered, taped to the inside cover is a handwritten note that says, PASSWORD: *DAVID AND TILLEY*.

Could I be this lucky?

I type in the words, and the screen opens to the desktop.

"Yes! I'm in."

I need to find the suicide note. I want to see when it was written.

I click on File Explorer. The quick access page comes up. Right below a row of folders she accesses frequently, which appear to be work-related because they're all titled with CarolinaVantage in the name. Then I find a lone document titled, I'M SORRY.

I stare at it for a moment, weighing my options. I know if I open it, there will be a record showing it was accessed at the time I opened it. I curser over the file icon, right-click, scroll down to properties selection, and click on it.

When the file information pops up, I snap a photo of it, thinking that before we leave, Jenna might be able to text Finster to ask if there's a way to reset the access stamp back to the original time. It's a long shot, but I file it away as a possibility.

I know there won't be time for that, but who makes a habit of looking at a file's property information anyway?

The key dates are when the file was created and modified. If I open the file, I should be okay if I don't make any changes.

I hope.

I hold my breath and open it.

It reads exactly like the kitchen printed copy—minus the signature.

It hits me that Tilly had handwritten the password taped inside the little black book.

I snap a photo of the password. Later, I will compare it to the signature on the note we found in the kitchen.

Like Jenna, I have a gut feeling that something doesn't add up.

As I put away the book, Jenna comes flying into the office.

"Someone's home." She mouths the words, and I freeze

until I hear the unmistakable sound of a door closing. I nearly come undone. It has to be the kitchen door that Jenna found unlocked earlier. My hand shakes so badly that it takes me a couple of tries to ex out of the email account.

But finally, I do, and I take care to close the computer screen quietly, returning it to the way I found it.

Footsteps sound on the hardwood. They're getting louder and closer, but Jenna is already opening the French doors behind me—the click of the deadbolt lock seems to echo through the house. She grabs me by the wrist and pulls me out the door. I don't even have a chance to scoot the chair back into place, but I manage to shut the door before the two of us sprint toward the car.

Somehow, Jenna already has the keys out and has remotely unlocked the doors. The two of us dive in and drive away.

We say nothing until we are on Interstate 26.

"I don't think anyone is following us," she says.

"I can't believe somebody came home," I say. "Do you know how close we came to being caught?"

"Who do you think it was?" Jenna asks.

"I have no idea. The footsteps sounded rather heavy, like a man's, but neither of us know Tilly's gait. Maybe she hasn't gone through with it yet."

"Maybe we should call the police and send them to the house?" Jenna says. "I'm still shaking. I'm pulling over."

As she steers the car off the highway at the next exit, I

call 911 and request a wellness check at Tilly's address.

By the time Jenna pulls into a fast-food restaurant and parks, I've given the operator a rundown of the situation and hung up.

Jenna is staring straight ahead. "I don't even know how to process everything," she says. "The note, the men's clothes, and the cologne that I'd bet were David's. And what was that save-the-date card?"

Both of us sit there silently.

Jenna shivers and rubs her arms. "I haven't even thought about Greg Paulson until now," she says. "What if Tilly is on her way to Greenville? Maybe that's why she wasn't home."

"But who was that in the house?" I ask. "I guess that's not important right now."

"I know it won't help things between you and Jack," Jenna says, "but I think you need to call him and let him know what we've learned."

My stomach lurches, but I know she's right.

"First, we try Greg's office again," I say. "If he's still alive, he can get somewhere safe."

"I'm on it," Jenna says. "You call Jack."

My heart is thudding.

I feel vaguely nauseated as I dial Jack's number, and then absolutely panicked when he answers on the second ring.

"Maddie."

Despite my utter terror at delivering the news, my body has a visceral reaction to his deep voice saying my name.

Before I can answer him, Jenna says, "The call went to Greg's voicemail again, but his voicemail box was full. This time, it wouldn't let me leave a message. I hope we're not too late."

Before she can say anything else, her phone rings. My heart leaps, hoping it's Greg calling her back.

She mouths, *it's Elizabeth Bennett* and gets out of the car to take the call.

"Hello?" Jack says. "Maddie, are you there?"

My entire body reacts to the sound of his deep timbre, but this is an emergency.

And he will be furious with me when he hears what I have to say.

"I'm here, Jack. I'm sorry to bother you, but there's an emergency."

I bring him up to date on Tilly's suicide note and tell him we've tried to reach Greg, but we weren't able to get through. I suggest he call the Greenville authorities as if he wouldn't do it without prompting.

I brace myself for him to lambast me, but instead, in a calm, measured voice, he asks, "Where are you?"

"That doesn't matter, Jack. Did you hear what I said? Tilly confessed to killing Kate. We need to warn Greg that Tilly is coming for him next."

"Maddie, Tilly Franklin and Greg Paulson are dead. Paulson's assistant found them in his office yesterday afternoon."

"Maddie, you and Jenna need to get yourselves somewhere safe. Now. Go home and set the alarm system, and do not open the door to anyone until you hear from me. Do you hear me?"

"If Tilly is dead, there's no danger," I say. "She admitted to killing Kate in her note."

"Maddie, someone tried to make this look like a murder-suicide, but we have a strong reason to believe it's not. For your own safety, I'm telling you this in confidence. There is a very real chance that you and Jenna could be in grave danger. Go home and stay home."

He disconnects the call.

I'm staring at my phone, trying to process Jack's words, when Jenna gets in the car.

My whole body is shaking, and all the horrific news that Jack told me spills out like word vomit.

Her eyes are wide, and she's shaking her head. "No. No-no-no-no-no." She locks the doors and looks around like she's afraid someone might come after us. "Elizabeth's news won't make you feel any better. I'll drive and talk because we need to get out of here." She starts the car. "Elizabeth said after she looked back at the notes and files she remembered Kate's case. She said Kate came to her for help because David Martin threatened to kill her, and the police weren't taking it seriously. Elizabeth helped Kate file for a restraining order. After that, she said that David Martin came after her. He followed Kate to one of her appointments and accused Elizabeth of brainwashing Kate and helping her invent things so the police would give her the restraining order. Elizabeth said he roughed her up enough that she pressed assault charges against him, and he was expelled from school. She told me when I came to see her that she thought this was the same case, but it had been so long ago, and he hadn't bothered her since, but she wanted to check her files before she said anything. She said the guy is unbalanced, and we need to be careful."

"But David has an airtight alibi. The police cleared him."

But then I do the math in my head. The story he told us at lunch made Tilly look unbalanced, but today, we found evidence that he lives with her—or at least stays there often. The save-the-date cards. The squirrelly way he acted at Kate's memorial.

"That suicide note," I murmur.

I pull out my phone and look at Tilly's signature in blue ink. Then I look at the elegant handwriting on the save-the-date cards and even the handwritten password.

"The handwriting on the suicide note isn't Tilly's," I say. "You were right. I don't think she wrote that note."

I remember what Jack said about Greg Paulson's assistant finding them yesterday.

I pull up the photo I snapped of the properties of the I'M SORRY document.

It was created this morning at 10:43 a.m.

"Tilly Franklin didn't write that suicide note," I say. "I have a sinking feeling I know who did."

Chapter Fourteen

~ *Jenna* ~

WE MADE IT back to the house in record time and in one piece.

After the shock of Jack's news on top of Elizabeth's warning about David, I must've spent the drive in a sort of fugue because all I can remember is being terrified that David would appear from out of nowhere and try and run us off the road or shoot out our tires.

That, and the two calls Mom made on the way home. One to London, who didn't answer. The other was to Gigi, who said, "Well, now you're just scaring me."

Mom told Gigi to sit tight and everything would be fine.

And it was.

We made it home safe and sound. We got inside and alarmed our fortress.

Gigi, Mom, and I are eating dinner when I get a text from London. I read it aloud.

"*Heeeeyyyy, baby girl! I'm back from Cabo, and I'm standing in your driveway. Don't keep a girl out in the cold.*"

"Oh, what a nice surprise, and how ironic," Gigi says. "Earlier today, I was thinking I wanted to ask her if she wanted to do a re-do of her wedding. After an appropriate amount of time passes, of course. But there's no better way to end all these curse rumors than to try again and have the beautiful event go off without a hitch."

I'm only half listening because I'm brain-dead after everything that's happened today, and I've been sitting here virtually scratching my head at the text's odd wording. London prides herself on using text abbreviations and hashtags. I don't think I've ever seen her use punctuation.

Before I can say anything, much less get up from the table, Gigi and Mom have turned off the alarm and opened the door to welcome her inside.

Before my foggy brain can catch up with what's happening, I see London standing there with a weird, dazed look.

"You're home." She sounds robotic, and her eyes dart from side to side.

Something is very wrong.

As Mom tries to pull London inside, David gets out of the red Ferrari parked in the driveway.

He's holding a gun.

I open my phone to call 911, but my hands shake so hard that I keep hitting the wrong numbers to open my lock screen.

"Hi, ladies, did you miss me? Stay right where you are, and everything will be fine. Jenna. Drop the phone and kick it out here to me."

I try one more time. If I can dial the numbers and connect the call before I drop it, the operator will send someone out.

David is standing on the porch now, pointing the gun at the back of London's head. She looks like she might faint.

Especially when he screams at me. "I said drop the phone, or I will shoot her and then shoot it out of your hand."

I have no choice but to comply. The phone with its lock screen photo of Ian and me sails to the right of David's foot, just out of his reach. He yanks London's head sideways to reach it and crushes the phone with his heel.

I pray that someone will be out, hear the commotion, and call the police. But I see no one.

I used to love how rural Mom's house was. Right now, I'm cursing the copse of trees and the berm on the far side of the mostly deserted street in front of her house.

"When I saw you running away from Tilly's place earlier today, I knew you'd figured things out."

"I don't know what you're talking about, David," Mom says. "What do you think we know that would make you resort to this?"

"I am not stupid, Maddie. Don't try to play games. You saw the save-the-date cards among whatever else you came to find. Don't patronize me. The jig is up—well, at least for you.

"It's a shame you had to leave so soon because we could've settled everything then. But I guess everything happens for a reason. I'd already set up a meeting with your good friend London, who wanted to talk to me about who killed Kate. You know, I told her I knew who the killer was. Surprise! It's me. Get inside." He grabs a fistful of London's hair and jerks her head back. "Now! All of you or I will put a bullet in her head."

As Mom, Gigi, and I move backward, David frog marches London forward.

"David, what are you doing?" Mom's voice is loud. "All I have to do is scream, and my neighbor will call the police. If you let us go, you'll have time to get out of here before the cops arrive."

For the first time in my life, I pray that Mrs. Wimberly is living up to her community busybody reputation, but please, Bertha, don't come out here yelling at us to pipe down.

She's prone to doing that, too.

David laughs. He slams the house door shut and locks it with his free hand. "There. That was easy, and it was pretty stupid of you. Let's set some ground rules right now. If you scream, all four of you will be dead before the police arrive, and I will still get away. Even if they catch me, I've already killed four people. What's four more?"

The choice is to scream, run, and die out in the driveway now, or die in the house later, because this psychopath is not about to let us go. Rounding us up will give him carte blanche to torture us. Figuratively or literally.

But every second we buy gives us that much more of a chance for the police to arrive.

Something else sticks in my mind. He said he's already killed four people. My tally is three. Kate, Tilly, and Greg.

Who's the fourth?

London is here, but Anson isn't. I hope it's not him.

I hope David has falsely inflated his body count. That's the least of our worries right now.

As he corrals us in the living room, Aggie and Homie, who I'm sure were cowering when David was shouting because they hate loud noises, start barking and acting tough.

Mom bends down to comfort them, but David screams, "Stand up and keep your hands where I can see them."

"David, please let me put my dogs in the other room," Mom insists. "Please don't hurt them."

If he does anything to those dogs, I will hurt him.

"Maddie, dear, I'm not a monster," David says in a soothing voice. "Those babies are safe and sound. I love corgis. Rest assured I will give them a good home after I take care of the unpleasant task I've come to do this evening. But first, let's have a little fun."

With the gun pointed at London's head, he tosses Gigi a roll of duct tape. I hadn't noticed until now that he'd been wearing it like a chunky bangle on his wrist.

He nods at me and says to Gigi, "Tape Jenna's hands behind her back and then tape her ankles together.

"And no funny business from any of you. If you do anything stupid, I will shoot all of you."

He looks back to Gigi. "Get to it. What are you waiting for?"

When Gigi wavers, he yells, "If you don't want to tape her up, I can always kill her."

Gigi whimpers and then starts picking at the place where the free end of the tape meets the roll. "I'm so sorry, honey."

She's shaking so badly, I'm afraid if David doesn't kill her, she might suffer a stroke.

"It's okay, Geeg," I say in a soothing voice. "Do what he says."

"Stop talking!" he yells.

As Gigi binds my hands behind my back, my peripheral vision catches movement at one of the transom windows in the living room. The house is built on a hill, so even though the window is at the top of the living room wall, from the outside, if you crouch down, you can look in.

Not only is the hinged window open—Gigi loves to crack windows to create a flow of fresh air throughout the house—I also see Anson's face peeking in. He presses his fingers to his lips in a universal *shhhhhhh* gesture and then ducks out of sight.

David's back is toward the window, so he doesn't see him.

If London and Mom saw him, they have good poker faces. Of course, Gigi is concentrating on tying me up.

A momentary wave of relief rushes through me. Help should be on the way.

And oh, my gosh. Oh, good. Anson is not dead.

I'm sure he's called the police. I hope so because now Anson is doing something else at the window. Something with a wire.

Is he trying to record what's happening?

He does help London with her vlog and livestreams. He knows how to do that kind of thing.

I think that's what he's doing now.

We need to get David talking.

And I need to stop looking at the window.

David is temporarily distracted because Gigi is having trouble tearing the tape that she's wound around my wrists, but he is also highly perceptive. If he catches me looking at the window, the best case would be that he would realize that the window is open, and he'd forgotten to close the drapes. The worst case would be that he would see Anson and kill us all before the police could arrive.

"I'm having trouble tearing the tape," Gigi says in a small voice.

"Use your teeth," David growls. "Do you think I'm going to give you scissors?"

I feel her forehead pressing against my forearms. I'm relieved when I feel the give of the tape. It's tearing easier than I feared it would. She gently helps me sit down on the sofa and begins binding my ankles together.

I feel for Gigi because she has to get down on her hands and knees to reach my feet and I know it's hard on her.

All the while, I think about getting David talking and do not even glance at the window.

"David, a few moments ago, you said you'd killed four people." I struggle to keep the fear out of my voice. "I know you killed Kate, Tilly, and Greg. Who's the fourth?"

For a moment, he beams as if I've asked him to list awards he's won or books he's written.

Then his face darkens. "Why would you ask that? The better question is, why would I tell you?"

"Because you said you killed four people. I'm curious about who the fourth might be," I persist and start praying that he won't shoot one of us and say, *That's who.*

"Curious like the cat. Bang, bang, kitty."

He inclines his head. "I'm going to kill you anyway, so I might as well tell you. It was Dana."

"Your alibi?" Mom asks.

David's gaze zings to her, as if he'd forgotten she was there.

"Yes, my alibi, Maddie. For the record, she was number two. Not number four. The police haven't found her yet. She lied. I wasn't with her the night of the murder. How could I have been? I was busy killing Kate."

He laughs like he thinks he made the cleverest joke.

Gigi is gaping at him. Her mouth is open like she's living a nightmare.

She is. We all are.

"What are you looking at?" he demands. "You have more work to do. Tie her up."

He gestures to Mom. A bereft-looking Gigi complies.

"I didn't tell Dana why I needed her to cover for me," David continues, clearly enjoying detailing his exploits. "I didn't have to. She just did it. For a while, she was obedient. Another woman with a soft spot for the ol' Dave-o. When they're in love with you, they do whatever you want them to do.

"The only problem was after the po-po paid her a visit and said they were investigating a murder, Dana started getting cold feet." He scrunches up his face like he's crying and makes his voice high-pitched. "I didn't know you wanted me to lie to the police. *Boo-hoo-hoo.*

"I had to draw the line when she wanted to go to the cops and rescind her statement—like I'd let her do that. Then, she was more trouble than she was worth. So…" He makes a gun with his free hand's thumb and index finger. "Pow! Night-night, Dana. Sleep tight."

His callousness sends shivers down my spine. Next, he has Gigi tape up London. Finally, he binds Gigi.

I know my grandmother is in shock, but as I watch him taping her wrists, I wish she would bust out some sick Taekwondo moves.

I make a mental note that mom, Geeg, and I will take Taekwondo classes to learn those sick moves after we get out of this mess.

When he makes Gigi sit down and starts binding her ankles, once again, his back is to the window. I steal a glance, but Anson is not there. I turn my face away but keep it so I can still sense movement in my peripheral vision, but I see nothing.

Anson, I hope you have a plan because I fear we're running out of time.

And where are the police? Why couldn't I have pulled out my phone fifteen seconds earlier and placed that 911 call?

"Ouch! You're hurting me," Gigi cries. "That's too tight."

"Shut up. You love to hear yourself talk, don't you? I bet you're in love with the sound of your voice."

Funny, David, I was thinking that about you when you were going on and on about Dana. So self-impressed.

I am furious, but my anger pales in comparison to the burning look on my mother's face. I know she will rip him apart with her bare hands if she gets the chance.

Wisely, Gigi is keeping her head down and isn't saying anything.

Finally, when he has us all bound and placed in different seats, spaced far enough away from each other so we can't set each other free, he says, "I need to go take a whiz. I won't be long. So don't do anything stupid. I'm taking my little friend with me." He holds up the gun. "When I get back, if you all aren't exactly where I've left you, it won't be pretty.

Capiche?"

No one answers, but we understand. After Gigi bound each of us, he checked to ensure she'd used enough tape and that it was bound tightly enough that we couldn't slip out. There wouldn't be enough time for us all to get free and get away.

Right now, it's either one or none.

Both dogs are leaning against Mom's legs. David eyes them before he leaves the room.

"Come on, mutts," David says. "I guess she had a point. We'd better lock you up."

He nudges them with the toe of his shoe, but they don't budge.

"Please don't hurt them, David," Mom says.

"Are you deaf?" he asks. "I told you I wouldn't harm them. Come on, dogs. Who wants to eat? You want treats? Come."

At the promise of treats, the traitorous animals trot along after him, and we hear doors open and shut.

"London," Mom whispers. "What are you doing here?"

"David contacted me and said he had information about Kate's killer that he wanted to share, and we needed to meet in person. He said he didn't want the reward money, but since I'd worked so hard on finding the killer through my Who Killed Kate vlog, he wanted to give me the info so that I could broadcast it right after the police arrested the murderer. He said he wanted you and Jenna to hear it, too, since you all had so much at stake with the murder happening at Gracewood Hall. I flew in from Cabo. He asked me to meet him here. I feel so stupid."

"Where's Anson?" Mom asks, but London doesn't have time to answer.

"What are you all talking about?" David says when he enters the room.

"David, we were wondering why did you kill Kate?" I say.

If I can get him talking again, it will buy us more time. Plus, if Anson's camera is rolling, we can record his confession. I hope we got what he said about Dana.

"Because, similarly to Dana, Kate deserved to die." He calls her a couple of ugly names. "However, unlike Dana, Kate had never been useful. She was the OG when it came to being more trouble than she was worth."

"I thought you were in love with her." I know it's not true, but it's a noncombative angle that might get him to tell us more. When he doesn't bite, I add, "I was so happy when I thought the two of you had found each other again. That true love had brought you together after all these years."

"There's no such thing as true love." His eyes are dark and cold. "Even if there was, I never loved her. She betrayed me. In so many ways."

"How?" I ask.

"Most recently, she was blackmailing me."

That little morsel lands like a grenade.

"Blackmailing you?" London says. "Over what?"

David points the gun at her. "Why are you so nosy? I could take you out right now, and I should. You are such a busybody with all the *Who Killed Kate* disingenuous solicitude."

"Yeah, I know you could kill me," London says. "So why not tell us? What do you have to lose? Tell us why she was blackmailing you. Wouldn't it feel good to get it off your chest?"

David flinches. His jaw is ticking. "I hate you almost as much as I hated Kate. I hated Tilly, too, but at least she brought something to the table. That's why I wanted to marry her."

"Wait a minute," Mom says. "You told us you wanted nothing to do with Tilly. You said she was the one pushing the marriage idea. That's what pushed you away."

"Yeah, I lied. I lied about a lot of things."

He laughs, and it's bone-chilling. It's the most diabolical sound I've ever heard.

"Tilly, God rest her soul—" He has the nerve to cross himself. "She came from a good family. Old money. Lots and lots of old money. Tilly was a good catch, but she had to complicate things by bringing Kate into the picture. That part of what I told you is true. Tilly hired Kate to be the maid of honor in our wedding. Tilly worked so much that she didn't have time to keep up with friendships. She decided to hire a bridesmaid. She didn't know what she was doing bringing Kate into the mix. No surprise there, but you don't have to be a genius to be born into money. She had no idea that Kate and I knew each other. I hadn't seen Kate in years, and suddenly, there she was, ready to ruin everything I'd worked so hard for."

"But why was she blackmailing you?" I ask.

"You guys are so nosy. But I suppose you won't give it a rest until I tell you. Will you?"

No one answers.

"I will take that as a no." David smirks. "It's kind of fun recounting everything. It's like looking back at vacation photos. Only, it's murder, and you'll just have to picture it in your little pea brains. Anyway, Tilly's family owned and operated CarolinaVantage Industries until recently, when they took the company public. They were getting ready to release their first-quarter earnings, which were tremendous, by the way. Tilly was excited and shared that information with me. She didn't know it, but by telling me that, she gave me the most fabulous gift—an opportunity to make bank on my own. It's one thing to marry into money, but it's a pride thing to make my own cash." He pounds his chest with his right fist and starts pacing. "When CarolinaVantage went public, the stock was low, but I knew that stock prices would skyrocket as soon as the earnings report was made public. I decided I'd cash in on the bottom floor. Buy low. Sell high. Investment 101, and I won't even charge you for that tip." David laughs again.

"Cut to the chase, David," Gigi says. "What does that have to do with Kate?"

Oh, no, Gigi, don't antagonize him.

This time, he turns the gun on Gigi. His face is red with rage, and he calls her a bad name. "Quit interrupting me."

"David, please, go on," I say, trying to calm him down. "I'm genuinely interested. I really believed you and Kate were in love."

Confusion flashes over his face and I fear he might not say any more.

Then he shakes his head. "When Tilly introduced me to her maid of honor, Kate and I were equally surprised to see each other, but neither of us said anything to Tilly. I guess we did have one thing in common. We both wanted the wedding to go on. For Kate, it was a business deal… And I guess for me, it was, too. By marrying Tilly, I would gain a fortune.

"But Kate got wind of my sharing the information about CarolinaVantage's earnings. She said she had stopped by my office to discuss what we wanted to tell Tilly about our prior relationship. I didn't know she was there, but she heard me on the phone with a client and video-recorded me as I gave him the scoop and placed the stock order.

"She managed to record me telling the client that he had to be quiet about the deal. A few days later, after CarolinaVantage announced their quarterly earnings and stock prices soared, Kate came back to see me and tell me what she knew. She showed me the video and was smug about having a copy of it stored somewhere on the cloud. She wanted one million, or she was going to report me to the Securities and Exchange Commission. When I told her I didn't have one million to give her, she said I could pay her twenty thousand in monthly installments.

"But she was bleeding me dry, and I couldn't exactly borrow the money from Tilly. To make matters worse, when Kate was in my office, delivering this bombshell, Tilly dropped in. So, she sees me and her maid of honor together—she still had no idea we knew each other—and she got suspicious. So, she hired Greg Paulson to follow us. Kate and I met once a month, but that was so I could deliver the money to her in cash. Not only was it becoming a real drain on my finances, but Tilly was ready to break up with me because she thought I was cheating on her with Kate. As if. I wouldn't touch that greedy pig.

"I wasn't about to lose my financial security because a woman from my past with a vendetta was trying to ruin my life. I followed Kate to the wedding at Gracewood Hall. I gave her twenty thousand and told her it would be the last payment."

That's the money that Sabrina said the police found in Kate's room.

"I'd already shelled out sixty grand. You'd think that would be enough to put an end to it, but, oh, no. She said I had to give her an additional fifty thousand by Monday. If I didn't, not only was she going to tell Tilly what was going on, but she was going to the police. I couldn't let her do that. She gave me no choice but to settle this matter once and for all." He shrugs like the matter was beyond his control.

"Did you take that bracelet off of Kate after you killed her and give it to Tilly?"

"Yeah. So? I was out of money, and I needed to give Till a little token to show my love. Plus, I figured it wouldn't hurt for the police to see it on Tilly's arm. You know, sowing the seeds of doubt. It was an insurance policy for myself."

"Was the suicide note another insurance policy?" I ask.

"Of course. That's how I'll get away with everything. Tilly confessed. Case closed. Now, I must take care of you before you ruin everything."

I want to tell him that he won't be able to make the police believe that Tilly killed us, but London says, "That was my bracelet. You took it off a dead woman's arm. You're despicable."

"And you're annoying."

David shoots London. He might've aimed at her heart, but blood is gushing from the area around her shoulder.

London, Gigi, Mom, and I all scream at once. My vision goes white and hazy around the edges as I brace myself for David to take us out, one by one.

Instead, in a surreal sort of slow motion with sirens in the background, the glass in the living room window blows out. For a split second, I think it was an explosion, but then

I see Anson land on David, taking him down.

The two struggle. The gun goes off. I close my eyes. I don't want to know if the discharged bullet hit someone because even though I'm struggling to free myself, I'm not having much success, and until I'm free, there's nothing I can do.

The next thing I know, someone fires a shot from the window that Anson crashed through. It hits David. The gun falls from his hand at the same time as what seems like the entire Hemlock police force and Asheville SWAT team crashes through the front door.

Epilogue

~ Maddie ~

Six months later…

"I NEED ALL the single ladies on the dance floor," the DJ says. "Calling all the single ladies. Please report to the dance floor pronto."

Anson and London got married today in front of a small crowd at Gracewood Hall. It's not the wedding extravaganza for five hundred that she had initially planned. There were fifty people in attendance, but that was the bride and groom's choice.

London asked that the staff and guests dress in 1940s Hollywood glam as a nod to Gracewood Hall's Carter and Linda Stanton history.

"I want our wedding to be totally retro," London said. "I want to do a bouquet and garter toss like my mom had at her wedding."

So, that's retro now?

Anson's sister, Betsy, is London's maid of honor and sole attendant. Betsy looks gorgeous in the blue dress she picked out herself from my shop for the occasion. There isn't a single bottle of Hermes *Vert Egyptien* nail enamel on the premises.

Betsy was happy to point out that today she's wearing the charm bracelet she left in Gracewood Hall. The one that led to her arrest for trespassing. We didn't press breaking and entering charges, of course. Because the mayor didn't want any more negative publicity, the town dropped the trespassing charges.

Gigi was happy to offer the place to London and Anson for their wedding. She said we needed a do-over to set us on the right track. Not that today's event erases the terrible thing that happened here, but at least having an official opening event at Gracewood Hall proves that the place is not cursed.

Yesterday, we made it through the pared-down rehearsal dinner without incident. The ceremony went off without a hitch, and now the reception is winding down.

I'll be honest, I'm holding my breath and uttering the intermittent prayer—please get us through this evening.

So far, so good.

Since recovering from being shot, London is a different person. Her role as a social media influencer is as solid as ever—in fact, I think she's gained a million followers. But now she seems genuine—on camera and off.

Maybe that's what a bullet in the shoulder and a brush with death will do to you.

Over the months since that fateful day, London had a long recovery and faced extensive physical therapy to regain the use of her left arm. She's doing great and wears her scar proudly. She and Anson have settled in Asheville, and we get together often.

Every time we do, it comes up that we are all lucky to be alive.

And we agree we wouldn't trade that luck for all the designer jewelry, fancy cars, or expensive champagne in the world.

If Anson hadn't taken that brave dive through the window to save the woman he loved, and if the authorities hadn't finally arrived when they did, some or all of us might not be here today. He said that almost losing London made him realize how much he loves her.

There's not a day that doesn't go through my mind.

I know all of us are hyperaware that we will not take a single day for granted.

David Martin was not so lucky, but his demise was of his own doing. Thank goodness he didn't die in my house. The ambulance took him to the hospital, where he was pronounced dead a few hours later.

As it turns out, Mrs. Wimberly had heard my loud exchange with David, and after surveying the situation through the bushes that separate our homes, she saw the gun, called the police, and reported what she saw. Anson had recorded David's confession, which allowed the case of who killed

Kate Asher to be closed without any doubts.

Ahh, Kate. Poor Kate. The one loose end we have is why Kate would stoop to blackmailing her ex. Was it a way to take back her power after David put her through such hell in college? Or was it a crime of opportunity?

I guess we'll never know.

But I do know that seeing how happy and in love London and Anson are and holding their wedding at Gracewood Hall feels like we've released the curse and exorcised the ghosts that might have haunted the place.

Gigi and Jenna are still living with me. I don't mind, really. Gigi is no trouble, and Jenna is putting on a brave front, pretending she's not at loose ends since Ian moved to Los Angeles. She's swamped with her business, which has gotten even stronger, thanks to some well-placed shout-outs from London on her social channels.

Ian has kept his promise to visit frequently. In fact, he flew in to be Jenna's plus-one for the wedding.

Jack and I ... we're rebuilding on a friendship foundation. I have no idea if the mayor was upset with him because the SWAT team had to be called in for us. We haven't talked about it, but he still has his job.

Also, we haven't talked about how both of us are still deeply grieving our late spouses. The good news is a few months ago, he and I started meeting for coffee at the Briar Patch again, like we used to. The weirdness that separated us is beginning to work itself out. The silver lining is I've had more time to write, and I finally managed to finish the book that had stalled during all the upheaval.

"Last call for the single ladies," the DJ says. "The bride is ready to throw the flowers."

I join Jenna and Gigi on the sidelines to give the contenders more room to catch the bouquet.

London is standing on the stage with her back to us. She makes a few fake moves but doesn't toss it.

Instead, she turns around. "Gigi, Jenna, Maddie, get over here. You're all single."

Thanks for pointing that out. Everyone is staring at us now.

"Come on," London says. "We're all waiting on you. Hustle your buns."

We wave her off.

"No, go ahead," I say.

She gives a London-like huff and petulant stamp of her foot before turning around and tossing the beautiful bouquet with the zest of an Olympic shot-putter.

The big ball of flowers flies over the knot of the catchers and hurtles straight for me. I have to raise my hands and grab the flowers or be hit in the face.

"Oh, my gosh. She did not just do that," I murmur.

"Better you than me," Jenna cracks.

I want to call for a do-over, but Anson is already on the stage hamming it up as he removes London's garter to a traditional burlesque song.

And wouldn't you know, Jack catches the garter.

Of course, he does.

I don't know whether to hide or run into his arms when the DJ calls for us to join London and Anson for a dance.

When the first strains of Nat King Cole's "Unforgettable" start and Jack offers his hand, I know there's still another chapter for us.

Our story isn't over yet.

Thank you for reading MAID OF DISHONOR, book 4 in the Wedding Bell Mysteries!

If you enjoyed this book, please consider writing a short review on Amazon or Goodreads.

Acknowledgments

Love and undying gratitude to the Tule Publishing team for believing in the Wedding Bell Mysteries. Sinclair – thank you for helping me make this book the very best it could be. Your sage input made all the difference in the world. I'm so lucky to work with you. Kelly, Mia, Julie, Jaiden, Meghan, and Maggie, thank you for your tireless work. I appreciate you all so much. Finally, to Jane Porter for your vision, perseverance, patience, and gentle (but mighty) soul. You make dreams come true. I am so proud to be part of the Tule family.

To my family for your unwavering love and support.

To Michael for your love and encouragement. You are my everything.

Sneak preview of SLAY BELLS RING – Book 1 in the Wedding Bell Mysteries cozy mystery series

~ *Jenna* ~

"A LITTLE TO the left," I say to Alicia Lopez, the assistant manager of my mom's shop, Blissful Beginnings Bridal Boutique.

Alicia came in early to get a jump on trimming the storefront windows, decking them out for Christmas. I'm standing outside on the sidewalk, helping her with placement of the decorations since my first appointment isn't until later this afternoon.

I'm an event planner. I operate my newly minted company, Champagne Wedding and Event Designs, out of an office in my mom, Madeline Bell's, shop.

Alicia pantomimes the question, My left or your left?

I hold up my hands to double check my directions, then point. "Your left."

She lugs the white and silver mesh reindeer into place between two bridal gowns we're showcasing amid a backdrop of twinkle lights and shimmery silver snowflakes.

"Perfect!" I say as I rub my hands together in a futile attempt to warm up. My wool coat is no match for the arctic blast that blew in this morning. If the Hemlock Today reporter gets it right, this is the start of a downward winter weather spiral. It's time to break out the parka.

I'm momentarily distracted from my hypothermia when Alicia flips the master switch and hundreds of white twinkle lights ignite. The sparkle and splendor of the bridal wonderland she has created warms me from the inside out.

"Oh! How pretty," Mom says as she joins me on the sidewalk in front of the shop.

"Isn't it?" I say. "Alicia is so creative. Look at the way she's draped the lights and snowflakes. The twinkling makes it look like falling snow."

We both sigh at the romantic picture she's created. Through the window, other gorgeous wedding gowns are visible, but the most beautiful of the lot are featured on sleek white mannequins scattered throughout the store. The other dresses wait on the built-in hanging racks for their perfect bride to discover them. There's a ballet-pink velvet Victorian chaise longue in the middle of the shop. It's draped with veils, blingy jewelry, jewel-encrusted shoes, and other accessories. Freestanding full-length mirrors, encased in ornate gold frames, reflect the crystal chandeliers and pale pink walls.

It's a shop fit for a princess.

"I can't remember the last time I had a date and this window makes me want to try on bridal gowns," I say.

"You're working way too much," Mom says. "You should be dating. Why aren't you dating?"

"By the way…" I make a show of looking at my watch. "It's nice of you to join us this morning, seeing how the shop opens in two minutes."

"I know. Sorry I'm late. I lost track of time."

"Too busy flirting with the chief?" I bat my eyes at her.

Mom's cheeks color. "Jenna, we don't flirt. He's just a friend and a good source for the police procedural elements of my books."

In addition to owning the bridal boutique, Mom is an aspiring cozy mystery writer. She hasn't published anything yet, but I have faith that she will. She works hard enough. Every morning before she opens the shop, she goes to the Briar Patch Bakery across the street and writes two pages of her book.

Jackson Bradley, Hemlock's new chief of police, has been an eager expert source. It's no wonder. Mom is a babe. She looks cute today in her puffer coat and cobalt blue tunic, which she's paired with black leggings and boots. She's pulled her dark hair into a low ponytail. It shows off her cheekbones.

"How is Studly Do-Right this morning?" I ask.

"Chief Bradley is fine." She gives me side-eye and pulls open the shop door.

I follow her inside.

Everyone knows the chief is interested in her.

In all fairness, I don't know that the chief realizes he's interested and my mother pretends to be oblivious. I'd love to see her happily in love. Of course, she doesn't want to talk about it. Even though it's been eight years since my dad's accident, she still considers herself married.

Plus, she's far more interested in dissecting my nonexistent love life.

"By the way," she says as she unlocks the cash drawer and puts the day's money in it. "Mrs. Gott asked me to convey her condolences. She's devastated that you're not marrying Riley Buxston."

She tries to deliver the line with a straight face, but she can't suppress a laugh when she sees my horrified expression.

"She's convinced you're not going to survive the weekend."

I roll my eyes. Riley Buxston and his fiancée, Grace Marie Taylor, are my clients. They're getting married tomorrow. Riley and I used to date, but that's ancient history.

"Why can't everyone mind their own business?" I ask.

"That's the beauty of small-town living," my mother says.

"Why do they assume that I'm torn up? It's ridiculous. I agreed to plan the wedding. I wasn't coerced into it. Does the Gossip Brigade think I'd take the job if I was heartbroken?"

"Maybe they think you're doing it so you can have the inside track for sabotage?" Alicia says as she pulls Windex and paper towels from the cabinet under the wrap stand.

I snort. "That's a great business plan. A surefire way to grow my client base." Then I sigh. "I hope the gossip hasn't gotten back to Grace Marie. I feel so bad for her."

"Do you think she's heard?" Alicia asks.

"I hope not," I say. "This nonsense just started a couple of days ago."

"Yeah," Mom says. "Isn't that when Grace Marie got into town?"

I cringe. "You're right. Why do people have to act so ugly?"

Since Grace Marie lived in Atlanta until this week, some considered her an outsider, despite Charles and Patricia Buxston pronouncing her good enough for their precious Riley.

The Buxstons were paying for the wedding. It would be an expensive and prestigious event.

Grace Marie's mother passed away when she was a teenager, and, according to Patricia, the bride's father doesn't have the means to throw the type of wedding Patricia wants for her son. So, Patricia and her husband, Charles, opened the vault. The stipulations were that the wedding had to be in Hemlock, not Atlanta; Patricia got final approval of everything, including Grace Marie's gown; and Grace Marie and Riley had to agree to move to Hemlock.

It was a lot of power to bargain away, but Grace Marie seems to be just as happy to turn over the decision making to

Patricia, who has made sure the wedding has all the proper touches. Added bonus, Grace Marie is off to a stellar start in the role of dream daughter-in-law.

At first, I was surprised that Patricia had hired me to plan the wedding—surprised, but grateful—the Taylor-Buxston wedding is Hemlock's social event of the year.

Soon, I realized that Patricia was making a point. She wanted me to know that this wedding could've been mine if I hadn't broken her darling boy's heart. It might have been annoying if she hadn't been so hilariously blatant about it.

"Just two more days and it will be over," I say. "But, right now, I need to call Patricia and touch base about a couple of things. Or should I call Grace Marie instead? If I sense any awkwardness about the recent gossip, it'll give me a chance to address it. Wouldn't it be awful to hear people gossiping about your husband-to-be and his ex-girlfriend? To know people think he should've married the ex, not you?"

"It's a good idea to call her," Mom says. "Get a read on the situation now so you can be proactive if need be. The good thing is, the Gossip Brigade will settle down after Grace Marie and Riley are married. They'll move on to something else."

I'm on my way back to the office to call Grace Marie when the bell on the door jingles.

"You have some explaining to do, Jenna Bell." Grace Marie's Southern accent drips venom, and her ice-blue eyes look positively murderous. Tall, athletic Riley slinks in behind her with a hangdog look on his face, as if this is the last place he wants to be but he can't escape his fiancée's invisible leash.

Obviously, she's heard the gossip.

"Good morning, Grace Marie." My smile feels too bright. "I was just about to call you."

In my peripheral vision, I catch Mom exchanging a look with Alicia.

"Let's go into my office where we can talk," I say to Grace Marie and Riley. Even if there are no other customers in the shop, I do not want my client to pitch a hissy fit on the sales floor.

I'm relieved when Grace Marie and Riley follow me past the racks of billowing tulle, lace, and satin. Grace Marie's angry footsteps are swallowed by the plush Persian rug that covers the hardwood floors.

"Would you like some coffee?" I offer as I shut the door behind us. The office I share with my mom isn't as fancy as the shop itself. In addition to our two desks, which are shoehorned in, the room is cluttered with boxes of brochures, complimentary bridal magazines, catalogues, and fabric samples.

Grace Marie wrinkles her pert nose and flounces. "I did not come here for a coffee chat, Jenna."

Her stylish, long wool coat looks brand new. I wonder if it's a gift from Patricia. The bloodred color matches her lipstick and is a striking contrast to her blonde hair and ivory complexion. Grace Marie may not come from money, but she is adapting well.

She lowers herself onto one of the chairs across from my desk. That's when I notice her hands are trembling.

"Grace Marie, what's wrong?" I ask in my most concerned voice. "How can I help?"

"What's wrong?" she sputters. "Are you kidding? If you want to help, stay away from my fiancé."

She's heard the gossip. Still, I play dumb.

"Excuse me?"

"You heard me." Grace Marie sniffles. Her eyes are brimming. "It's pretty low for the wedding planner to move in on the groom, don't you think?"

"Grace Marie, Riley and I are just friends. I am not interested in your fiancé."

I glance at him for backup. But he's sitting slumped forward in the chair, his elbows braced on his knees. His attention is fixed on the floor.

Come on, Riley, man up.

"Riley, will you please tell your fiancée there is nothing between us."

Finally, he lifts his head and looks at me. He has the nerve to look wounded.

It takes everything I have to not yell, He's all yours, Grace Marie. I had my chance. He proposed to me years ago. I didn't want to marry him then and I don't want him now.

Instead, I prod, "Riley?"

"There's nothing going on, Grace Marie," Riley says in a robotic monotone. It's the voice of a man who has uttered these words countless times to deaf ears.

I'd wager Grace Marie picked out his expensive preppy clothes—khaki chinos and hunter green cable-knit sweater peeking out from his navy pea coat. They belie the dark circles under his eyes, which make him look as if he hasn't had a good night's sleep in weeks. His blond curly hair looks a mess, like it hasn't seen a comb in days.

That's the Riley I know.

Grace Marie turns her weepy gaze on Riley. "Am I supposed to believe you? Why would everyone in town say you should be marrying Jenna if there wasn't some truth to it? I just don't understand why they'd do that."

"Actually, Grace Marie, I have several ideas why." I know she's not asking me, but Riley isn't even trying to get through to her. "You take a few hopeless romantics who have watched too may Lifetime TV Movies, mix in a bushel of sour grapes because they weren't invited to your wedding—because you do realize your wedding is Hemlock's social event of the season, don't you—fold in the small-town mindset that wishes Hemlock's most eligible bachelor would've picked a hometown girl, and you've got a recipe for…this. But he chose you, Grace Marie. He wants to marry you. When you and Riley get home from your honeymoon, it will stop. I promise you it will."

She squints at me and tilts her head to the side, reminding me of my mother's corgis.

She nods, but then her eyes brim again. "I just have one thing to say to the two of you. Don't make a fool out of me. If there's something I need to know, just say it."

"Honey, there's nothing going on between me and Jenna. I don't know what else to say to make you believe me."

Grace Marie is studying him with watery eyes.

I hand her a tissue.

"I mean, sure, we loved each other once—and I'll always kind of love her, but—"

Grace Marie wails. At the top of her lungs.

She starts full-on sobbing.

Riley gives me an exasperated look. "I don't know what else to say."

He slumps back in the chair, crosses his arms over his chest, and stretches his long legs out in front of him.

A knock sounds on the door and my mom peeks in before I can answer. "Everything okay in here?"

Grace Marie swipes at her eyes with the tissue and turns her back to the door.

"We're fine," I say. "Just working through some last-minute concerns."

Mom's gaze darts from me to Grace Marie to Riley and full circle back to me. She's mentally telegraphing, *Do you need help?*

I shake my head and force a smile. "The bride has some questions before the big day tomorrow."

My mother mouths, "Let me know if you need help."

I nod. "Mom, do you have customers?"

It dawns on me that maybe this is her subtle way of letting me know the sound of backroom keening doesn't inspire other brides to say yes to the dress.

"We will in a half hour."

I give her a thumbs-up. She disappears, leaving the office door cracked open a couple of inches. Probably so she can save me if Grace Marie tries to kill me.

I turn back to my clients.

"Grace Marie, I think what Riley means is that we can't change the past, but his future is with you. Right, Riley?"

"Sure," he says. "You are my future, Grace Marie. You are my life."

I wince. Again, he doesn't sound convincing. When he reaches out to take Grace Marie's hand, she pulls away, her two-carat diamond glinting under the office lights. She must notice it, too, because she stares at her hand, straightens the ring, and sighs.

It sounds more like a sigh of appreciation than one of resignation.

It calls to mind something my mother shared when Riley proposed to me all those years ago.

She said, "Even the best marriage is challenging. You can't just love the person. You have to like him if you're going to make it through the ups and downs. A good test is to look at your relationship at the moment of the proposal.

Are you happy enough to build a marriage on that particular moment, because it's likely the most romantic of the relationship?"

Basically, she was saying it was all downhill from there.

Mom hadn't meant it that way, of course. It was simply her way of saying romantic love doesn't last, but a strong foundation of trust and admiration does.

After that, I couldn't marry Riley. Not only were we too young, back then neither of us had a clue about where we were going or what we wanted out of life. Riley Buxston came from a wealthy family, and he'd never had to work a day in his life. It wouldn't have been a marriage of equals. I would've been the one steering the ship. When I thought about spending the rest of my life with someone, it wasn't what I wanted.

Is it what Grace Marie wants?

But it's not my concern. My role is not to play marriage counselor, but to plan the perfect wedding and make sure everything goes off without a hitch. Never in my life did I dream I'd have to factor in small-town gossip as a possible snag.

"Grace Marie, it's normal to have pre-wedding jitters. I think that's what's causing you to feel this way."

"Don't tell me what I'm feeling," she snaps. "If I could fire you, I would. But I can't. Patricia hired you. She loves you. And because of that, I have to listen to all the gossip and deal with people whispering about you and Riley behind their hands."

Grace Marie chokes on her words. Her chest convulses. I want to assure her that Patricia doesn't love me, that she's taking great pleasure in the fact that I'm not the bride, but it won't help.

"How long have you and Riley been together?" I ask.

Grace Marie blinks and sniffs. "Two years."

"Okay, consider this. If he and I had been destined for each other, we had five years to work things out before he even met you."

Grace Marie blinks again, but this time she appears to be considering what I'm saying.

"Do you know how many times he and I went out during the five years before you two met?"

"How many?" Her voice sounds small.

"Zero. Riley and I have not even seen each other casually as friends in the time since he and I broke up. Doesn't that prove there isn't anything between us?"

Grace Marie is staring at her ring again.

"I guess not." Tears stream down her face.

"Jenna's right, Grace Marie." Riley has finally found his voice. He turns to his bride. "I love you."

The words sound right, but Riley looks downright terrified, like he would run if he could.

"It's just so hard to know all those people are talking about the two of you," Grace Marie says. "It's so disrespectful. So hurtful."

I hand Grace Marie another tissue. "I'm sorry you're having to endure it. It is hurtful and disrespectful. But, Grace Marie, I'm on your side. Don't let them rain on your wedding. The best response is to arrive at the church with your head held high and show them that not only are you the most beautiful bride they've ever seen, but you're the only bride for Riley Buxston."

Grace Marie's face softens. She blows her nose. "I guess you're right. If you were still in love with Riley, I'm sure you wouldn't be so eager for us to walk down the aisle. I'm sorry, Jenna."

Riley is staring at the floor again.

But Grace Marie doesn't seem to notice. She stands up and hugs me. I recognize the perfume she's wearing. It's one of the more potent Chanel fragrances. I don't know which one, but it's the same one Patricia wears.

I find it creepy that Grace Marie would want to smell like her mother-in-law, but hey, who am I to judge? Maybe she helped herself to a squirt of Patricia's perfume?

Ehh…still creepy.

"It's okay," I assure her. "The Gossip Brigade is one of the hazards of living in Hemlock. They get their minds fixated on something and they can't give it up. They're like pit bulls with a bone. Just ignore them."

"I wish we could move to Atlanta," Grace Marie says to Riley. "Let's just go. Right now. Let's elope."

"You know we can't do that," Riley says. "I don't have a

job there. My dad's company is here. I have to work."

"Why can't you work remotely?" Grace Marie whines.

They're talking as if I'm not here. I consider that a good thing.

"We've already been over this, Grace Marie. I'm working out of the home office. Dad says we can talk about expanding my territory to include Atlanta in a year. In the meantime, I've got to prove myself."

The first time Riley worked for his dad's company, things didn't end well. Charles Buxston fired his son and cut off his allowance. That's when Riley moved to Atlanta and met Grace Marie.

Patricia delighted in rubbing my nose in the fact that Riley's job with Buxston-Fox Development and the condo the Buxstons had given them were engagement presents.

"Why is Atlanta so important to you now?" Riley asked. "You hated your job. If we live in Hemlock, you won't even have to work."

Grace Marie takes a deep breath and exhales loudly. It sounds as if she's fighting against slipping back into her funk. I wonder if she's starting to realize that the bling, the new clothes, the condo, and the promise of a life of leisure come at a high personal cost?

As if steeling her resolve, she clasps her hands together, making a clapping sound.

"Okay, this is how it's going to be," she says. "Riley, I need you to ask your mother to put an end to these horrible rumors. Patricia has a lot of influence around here. Make her do something. Because if we're going to live here, I want this nonsense to stop. And I mean now. Otherwise, I can't be responsible for what I'll do to the next person I hear talking about me—or you and Jenna. Do you understand me?"

Her voice catches. The tears are back. They're flowing down her pretty face causing her mascara to run, making her look maniacal.

Riley nods and pulls her into his arms. Then he kisses her. Her body relaxes into his. The kiss grows deeper and goes on longer than is comfortable for a bystander with a front-row seat. I turn around and study my project board. Looking, but not really seeing what's written on it. I don't turn back around until I hear Riley mutter, "Don't cry, Grace Marie. I love you."

Intermittent kissing breaks up the words. "I really do love you," Riley coos. "I don't know how you put up with me."

More kissing.

"I don't know why I put up with you either," she says. "But I love you, too… And it's a good thing—" Grace Marie's voice is breathy between the words and the kissing. "Because as much as I want to be your wife, Riley Buxston, sometimes I want to kill you."

About the Author

Award-winning and USA Today Bestselling Author Nancy Robards Thompson has worked as a newspaper reporter, television show stand-in, production and casting assistant for movies, and in fashion and public relations. She started writing fiction seriously in 1997. Five years and four completed manuscripts later, she won the Romance Writers of America's Golden Heart award for unpublished writers and sold her first book the following year. Since then, Nancy has sold more than 50 books and found her calling doing what she loves most – writing mysteries, romance, and women's fiction full-time.

Thank you for reading

Maid of Dishonor

If you enjoyed this book, you can find more from all our great authors at TulePublishing.com, or from your favorite online retailer.

Made in United States
Troutdale, OR
08/18/2024